Frayed Around The Edges

Anthony Bunko

All the characters in this book are fictitious, and any resemblance to peculiar people, repugnant creatures or Lois the Horny Virgin Slayer is purely coincidental. This book is also available with asbestos pages for reading inside ovens or next to the fires of Hell or on a beach in Noosa.

ISBN:- 9798647954961
First published 2020 by STRUMMMER PUBLISHING
Email:- anthonybunko@hotmail.com

Dedicated to: -

All the misplaced souls

concealed in the undergrowth

My nan used to be a werewolf!!

List of the TALL tales in this book

Chapter: -

1. *Fate*
2. *Click*
3. *Scollop*
4. *Buzzin'*
5. *Flowers*
6. *Nightmare*
7. *Home*
8. *Promise*
9. *Sin*
10. *Chance*
11. *Bottle*
12. *Victor*

Never cry wolf on a Tuesday

FATE

S L A M

My eyes shot open. My head groggy and my neck stiff from lying awkwardly on the cold floor. I slowly got to my feet. I tried to steady myself on a pair of legs that felt like rubber bands. I had to lean against the metal wall to keep myself from falling over.

What the hell?

My eyes scanned the strange and unfamiliar surroundings. It looked like an old-fashioned 1950's style elevator; the type found in some cool, high-class hotel in uptown New York. The design was peculiar; very ornate, yet dark and eerie. Four ugly looking gargoyles stared down at me from each corner. There were no handles to open the door, or buttons to push.

How did I get here?

Where were my friends?

The last thing I remember was being in the night club with Jez and Max. Jez scored some pills, lots of them. Well, it was my birthday! We dropped a couple in the toilet just before they "forced" me to drink several shots, one after the other. The place soon came alive, buzzing; the music rattled my entire body. I watched a couple of hot girls grinding each other on the dance floor. The hairs on the back of my neck standing to attention like guard soldiers on parade.

But where the fuck was I now?

Was this some kind of birthday prank?

'Jez. Max. Stop messing around. Let me out' I yelled as loudly as I could.

Silence.

More images filled up my head. A shiver raced down my spine and smashed head on into my brain. I recalled Jez handing me two or three more small, purple tablets. He winked at me. 'Happy birthday Billy, I love you man.' He hugged me.

What a thoughtful friend. I hugged him back before popping them in my hungry for more thrills and pills mouth. The rush hit me instantly. My head spun so fast I became dizzy. The beat of the music and flashing lights blended into one. I was absolutely buzzing, enjoying life. But then, but then … I felt peculiar. A cold flush engulfed my entire body even though I was sweating all over.

I tried to catch Jez's attention but he was too busy trying to pick up some short-haired girl in a yellow mini skirt. I could feel the colour draining from my face, my lips dry; my tongue sticky. Goose pimples like black, hairy spiders wearing hiking boots, marched all over my body. Air. I needed air. I staggered towards the exit.

Then the blackness.

The darkness.

The silence.

Why was I in the lift, alone? What happened? I don't remember seeing an elevator in the club. I didn't think the club had a second floor? I concentrated hard as I paced around the small, confined space. I sat back down in the corner. My breathing heavy. My hands trembling. Suddenly, the noise of the elevator engine made me jump. I could hear the pulley wheels engaging and then the elevator slowly started to move downwards. A tension wrapped itself around my entire body tightly and refused to let go.

The lights flickered on and off before going out completely. Pitch black. I could still feel the elevator moving down. A slow, purring noise like a mechanical cat getting stroked on an old woman's knee.

BOOSH

It stopped.

'9.35pm' illuminated above the exit. I readjusted my eyes as the doors opened and an onslaught of bright light blinded me. Mesmerised and confused I walked towards the exit.

BANG!

I walked face first into a pane of clear glass which stopped me from leaving the confines of the lift. Outside, bizarrely, I could see the inside of the nightclub. The house lights on. People stood about in silence, shock expressions on their faces. I saw Jez and Max kneeling over someone stretched out on the floor. I could make out a pair of legs.

'Those shoes look familiar,' I thought. 'Just like mine.'

I looked down and I suddenly froze. They *were* my shoes! I staggered backwards, bumping hard against the back wall. Trying to regain composure, I moved back to the front and put my ear against the glass, hoping to figure out what the hell was happening.

'Billy … Billy,' Jez slapped my face. Not my face exactly, the face of the other me lying unconscious on the ground. 'Wake up … please.'

'He's dead! He's dead!' some girl screeched and raced around hysterically.

'I'm not dead, I'm not dead … I'm over here … look … I'm here!' I banged my fists against the glass barrier. No one could hear. No one could see me standing there, watching them all.

'Come on Billy, wake up … wake up.' It was Max this time.

A bouncer barged his way through the crowd and checked my pulse. Max looked at Jez, a worried expression on his face. 'What have you fuckin' given him!' the bouncer screamed at Jez, who in return just shrugged his shoulders, tears filling his eyes. 'It's too late to cry now tough guy,' the bouncer snapped, 'What have you fuckin' given him?'

'Just a few tablets.' Jez's voice shook, 'It's his birthday.'

'You kids will never fuckin' learn.'

He motioned for a woman behind the bar to call 999. Pandemonium broke out but in very slow motion. Girls screamed, in sluggish and deep, monstrous voices. Jez's face frozen like a waxworks dummy. Max plonked himself down on a chair and sat in silence, head in his hands.

I stared in horror at the body lying on the Night-club floor; at MY body lying on the Night-club floor. I let out a scream as the lights faded, and the lift jerked and dropped downwards again.

A few minutes later the paramedics hurried in. Quickly checking me over and talking amongst themselves. One of them placed an oxygen mask over my face. They gingerly lifted me onto the stretcher. My friends followed them, and me, exiting via the front of the club.

'Wait!' I screamed, pounding my right fist as hard as I could, trying to bust the glass. 'Wait! Where are you taking me? Damn it!' I screamed louder. But as soon as they were out of sight, the elevator started to move again. It went dark for a third time. The only thing I could hear was my heart beating way down in my chest. I was too scared to panic or contemplate my fate.

After what seemed an eternity the elevator stopped. This time '10.41' illuminated above the door before it opened once again. The front room of my house this time. My dad sat on the couch flicking the button on the TV remote as usual. My birthday cards were on display above the fireplace. My mother brought in two mugs of coffee and sat down next to him. I found myself smiling at how happy they looked. But that image was soon shattered.

There was a knock on the door. A puzzled look appeared on both their faces. My mother went to answer it. A moment later, she reappeared crying hysterically, two policemen stood behind her. My father jumped up; the hot coffee spilled over the rug.

'What's wrong, Officers?'

'It's Billy, it's Billy,' my mother piped up.

'It's your son, Mister Jones.'

Before I could hear the rest, my father accidentally pressed the volume button up on the television set. The voice of Graham Norton interviewing some overweight American actor with great teeth drowned out what was being said. I watched them get their coats and trudge out of the door. My mother gripped my father's hand tightly.

Darkness yet again. I assumed I was now travelling between floors to a different time. A minute later, another floor with another time above the door. A hospital waiting room. Jez and Max sat in silence. A boy with a smashed-up nose was arguing with a nurse in the far corner of the room.

'I've killed him Max, I've killed him,' Jez muttered.

'Don't be so stupid, he'll be OK,' Max said, more in hope than optimism.

'What if he dies? I've known him since we were three. We grew up together. What if he dies? What am I going to tell his mam and dad?' Jez turned and punched the chair.

The boy with the mashed-up face stopped shouting and sat down.

'Look, he's not going to die,' Max added.

Jez started to cry. Snot ran from his nose. He wiped it on his shirt sleeve and yelped, 'I love him man, what am I going to do?'

Max reached across to pat his shoulder.

I turned my head at the sound of squeaky footsteps coming down the hallway. The footsteps belonged to a young, fresh-faced boy wearing a white coat and trainers. He carried a clipboard.

'I'm Doctor Manning,' he spoke, 'are you Mr Jones's friends?' His voice had a soft edge to it, but seemed to somehow belong to a much older and wiser man.

They both nodded. From behind the glass, I found myself doing the same. He stared straight at them and continued, 'Do you know what Mr Jones has taken?'

I watched Jez put his hand in his pocket and pull out a handful of purple pills. 'These.'

'Where did he get them from?' The doctor took them off him.

Jez hesitated before admitting he had given them to me.

'What are they?'

'I don't really know.'

The doctor shook his head. Before he departed, he turned and added purposely, 'Call yourself a friend?'

Max jumped up. 'Will he be all right, Doc?'

'He has not regained consciousness yet, only time will tell. It's not looking good.' He walked away.

I looked on in horror. I felt as though I had been smacked around the head by a baseball bat, swung by one of the New York Yankees. I couldn't feel my legs. Why was this happening to me? I was only 16, well, I had just turned 17 actually.

'Don't let me die!' I screamed, knowing it was going to go unheard by the doctor and Jez. Praying it wouldn't go unheard by God.

The door at the front of the room swung open and my parents rushed in. 'Mam! Daaa…' I called out, but my words trailed off when I saw Father Clancy just behind them.

Without warning, the floor beneath me gave way completely. I fell down and down, deeper into darkness. Spinning and toppling through the air I yelled out at the shadows.

Silence.

I closed my eyes tightly waiting for certain death.

BOOSH!

I landed on a big stockpile of discarded boxes. The breath returned to my body. I slid down from the pile onto the ground and got to my feet. A large billboard in front of me flashed brightly against a musty backdrop. *'This way, Billy'* an arrow flashed.

I inhaled a mouthful of breath. The surrounding air felt much warmer. It felt hot and sticky, wrapping itself around my body as it burned into my nostrils. Off in the distance somewhere, I could make out the distinctive sound of a large insect chirruping away; the sad song of the male cicada was strangely soothing to my otherwise disturbed state of mind. It remained sinisterly dark, but my eyes soon adjusted to the lack of light. I could make out shapes standing motionless in the shadows. Red, demonic eyes illuminated brightly in front of me … teasing and taunting … then, as quickly as the eyes became visible, they disappeared.

'*Fresh meat…fresh meat,*' words shot out from the darkness, followed by hilarity.

'*Let's just have him,*' someone, or something, whispered hoarsely behind me. I could feel their balmy breath near my ear. I turned sharply, but no one was there. The sound of snickering rose up to meet me just before a globule of spit landed on my cheek. I wiped it off with my hand, throwing the green gooey substance to the ground.

'*Come on, he won't be missed,*' the same demonic voice hissed.

'*Yes, yes, fresh meat,*' another chipped in.

'*We can't ... not yet ... you know the rules!*' an even deeper voice rose up, and then sniggered, '*But druggy boy, you will be ours sooooon.*'

A powerful kick connected with my thigh. '*We're going to make your death ... Hell.*'

Several different, distinct voices made up the wicked choir mocking me. The catcalls continued but then stopped abruptly. Back to silence except for the sound of my footsteps as I walked on, trying to stay focused.

'What the fuck?'

I froze when the ground underneath my feet slowly started to move. I didn't want to look down, but my eyes were irresistibly drawn to the squirming floor beneath my feet. Thousands of long, slimy snakes slithered around my ankles. I screamed and tried to kick them away. Laughter echoed all around. Then the creatures disappeared as well.

Another whisper in my ear made me spin around sharply, my heart racing. 'It's bloody hot in here,' said a half-roasted pig on a spit balancing over a campfire. 'Can you smell something burning?' the animal continued conversationally, while sniffing at the air.

I looked around for some end to this madness. In the distance loomed a large building covered in lights. I rushed towards it; the squealing noise made by the poor pig embedded in my mind.

As I reached the enormous door, a man in a neat, expensive suit greeted me. 'Hello Billy, we've been expecting you.' He led me to a rather stylish looking chair next to a very large roulette table and wheel.

An even more bizarre array of people sat around that table, not making eye-contact with each other. They came in all shapes and sizes, colours and ages. Myself included, I counted at least twelve faces gawking at the huge gaming wheel. All of the seats were occupied except one on my left-hand side. I was mystified. Where the hell was I now? Could the bizarre scene get any freakier? I was almost too afraid to ask.

A small commotion from the end of the room broke out and disturbed my thoughts. A tall, athletic man entered and took the last remaining seat. An Asian boy, who was sitting by his parents and his younger sister rushed over and asked the new arrival for his autograph.

'That's Danny McBride,' said the old woman in the seat next to me. 'He's the new goalkeeper for Leicester City,' she added majestically.

I'm not sure how the hell someone of her age would know that, but I thanked her for supplying me with that much needed titbit of information. She smiled back at me. I withdrew sharply on seeing the hideous sore taking over one side of her once beautiful features. She looked down at the floor, disappointment evident on her sad face with its deformed features.

‘Welcome, Ladies and Gentlemen,’ announced the smartly dressed croupier, who suddenly appeared like a genie from a bottle. ‘I would like to thank you all for coming along tonight; some of you at such short notice.’

He produced a red rose from the inside of his jacket and handed it to a pretty, but pale looking girl sitting on his left-hand side. He continued, ‘Tonight we only have six spins of the wheel. That’s only six chances to change your life forever.’

‘I feel lucky tonight,’ the old lady informed me and squeezed my hand tightly. ‘I’ve been coming here now for the last couple of weeks and I haven’t won anything yet. Not even close.’

I could hear and almost feel the dejection in her words.

The croupier explained the rules of the game. ‘There are thirteen spaces on the roulette wheel.’ He spun it round and around. ‘Everyone will be asked to pick a numbered ball from the bag that Angela has.’ A beautiful woman in a bikini paraded around in front of us. We all picked a ball from the silky, black bag. I picked number two. I didn’t show anyone my number. I’m not sure why.

‘Have you all got a number?’ he asked. We all nodded. ‘Well, let's hope it's your lucky day.’

After what I had just been through, I didn't feel lucky at all. I still didn't know what was going on! I still didn't know what I was doing here amongst this strange band of losers! Maybe it was some kind of Game-Show. A Game-Show where the winning contestant sits by a conveyor belt and tries to remember as many objects as possible in sixty seconds. 'Cuddly Toy!, Food Processor, Cement Mixer,' I almost laughed to myself.

'Let the games begin!' the man smirked.

Out of the blue, a drum roll exploded. Another pretty girl spun the wheel in an anti-clockwise direction. The plain white ball tossed and turned, and bounced onto the playing surface to start its journey toward finding a place to lay its plastic head. It skipped and jumped around, unable to make up its mind. We all sat mesmerised by its movements. We gasped as it finally settled in the number seven position.

'Number seven' the caller yelled out like a carnival speaker inviting an audience in to see the Freak show.

All eyes darted from their own ball to each of the other contestants. A rather well-to-do gentleman slowly held his ball up, his hands shaking.

‘Well done Sir,’ the caller said, ‘Mr Long, isn’t it?’ The gentleman nodded. ‘Please can you go with the lovely Angela; she will look after your every wish.’

She led the old man towards an extremely grand looking door located at the far end of the room. As the door crept open, I could just make out lots of people milling about inside. A thick, red carpet lined the floor and a brightly-lit chandelier sparkled above their heads.

That quick snapshot of the victory enclosure whetted my appetite for winning at least one of the last five places. That’s where I wanted to be. I gripped my ball tightly. I really didn’t want to go back past the horrible demon things outside.

I crossed my fingers. By the time I looked back to the confines of the gambling table, the number seven space had been switched off. A new game was already underway.

The next number to be called was the number one. I searched about for the lucky winner of the second roll of chance. Strangely; a small, deformed baby’s hand poked out of an old-fashioned baby carriage. It clutched both a rattle and the correct numbered ball in its fingers. Angela wasted no time in taking the ball, unlocking the brakes of the stroller and pushing the infant through to the winner's compound.

'No age limit to this contest I see,' I muttered to the old lady next to me. She wasn't really listening. I had the odd feeling that it would only get stranger.

I smiled at the pretty girl who had received the flower earlier. As she smiled unconvincingly back, I noticed the bandages around her wrists, and the bottle of sleeping tablets that she had been feeding on.

'Number eleven' the caller cried out.

'YESSSSSSSS,' a scream bellowing out beside me nearly made me fall off my stool. The little old lady with the mangy face quickly raised her arm to show the rest sitting around the table that she had the magical numbered ball.

'Well done … well done.' I congratulated her.

Although her winning meant another ball gone, I was genuinely pleased for the lady I had just met. Perhaps now she could get a doctor to examine that nasty wound which was obviously affecting her quality of life.

'Pray hard and you will win as well,' she said before kissing me on the cheek. I recoiled from her and wiped the wetness with my sleeve. 'I'll keep you a seat next to me in the big room,' she added before disappearing through the door, as happy as a child going to see Santa. She never looked back.

I closed my eyes and to be honest, I did say a little prayer to the man upstairs. I hadn't really done that for a long time. I concentrated hard. The image of my parents dressed all in black, standing around a coffin kept popping into my brain. I could feel the life slipping away from me.

'Come on Number 2 … Come on!' I muttered to myself as I watched the wheel spin around and around. 'Shit.'

Next number out, Number 5, went to another old lady who was quickly ushered away.

'Ladies and Gentlemen there are only two more rolls to go,' the croupier informed us. I gripped my counter even tighter. The next ball danced on top of the compartments on the wheel and then somehow came to rest on four different spaces at the same time.

'Numbers four, twelve, ten and six,' roared the caller.

'What's going on?' I wondered.

'This thing is fixed!' I stood up to protest when I saw the Asian family all get up at the same time.

'What's the chances of that? It must be a miracle!' I sat back down and whispered to the girl in bandages.

She ignored me and swallowed another couple of her coloured tablets. I watched the happy family skip merrily towards the door. I wished it was my parents and I going on that trip, but I had never been really lucky in life. Just my luck.

Now it was crunch-time. Last roll, last chance. I stared at the four people left. The wheel turned slowly. The white ball moved more mischievously this time, taking great pleasure in springing in and then out of all the surviving spaces. It moved around the wheel for the final lap and bounced between the numbers two and three. Two, no, three, no, two, wait … three. The ball found its final resting place on someone's fateful number three.

'Oh no! Trust my fuckin' luck!' I jumped up, and yelled miserably. I threw my ball down onto the floor, the loser again.

As expected, it was the good-looking goalkeeper who held up the right numbered ball in his massive goalkeeper hands.

'Trust him,' I said under my breath. 'He knew he was going to win it. Bet he wins everything and I bet he's got a gorgeous, model wife and perfect kids.'

I swore to myself several times as I watched him follow Angela into the room. The room I wanted to be in.

What now? I looked about. I really didn't want to go back the way I had come. I had a really bad feeling about it. I wanted to go through the big door; it looked safe and warm, and happy in there.

'Hard luck, ladies and gentlemen,' the caller droned, 'but we will see you all again. Don't worry your time will come!'

A giant puff of dark grey smoke covered the entire room. I opened my eyes. I lay in a hospital bed. Nurses busily rushed around me.

What the hell? Where was I now? What about the roulette game?

I looked across the ward. Most of the occupants lay asleep or talking to visitors. In the far corner, a television set spoke to itself. My mouth was dry. I took a sip of water. Suddenly, a breaking news flash caught my attention. The reporter stood by the side of the road at the scene of a horrendous car crash. It appeared that a BMW had smashed head-first into a tree. I dropped the cup when I saw the image of the new goalkeeper of Leicester City appear in a small box in the corner of the screen with the caption underneath: 'Danny McBride, 1994 – 2019'.

My blood ran cold. My heart began to pound loudly in my chest. I turned to the bed next to me. I almost screamed. In it, fast asleep, was the girl from the roulette wheel. She still had the bandages on her wrists. A bottle of tablets and a single red rose stood on her bedside table. The respirator by her side indicated that she was doing fine. Another image on the TV screen forced me to watch more. A fire in the centre of Bristol had killed an entire Asian family. A photograph of a little boy and his sister - the same kids I'd just seen with their family cheerfully passing through those big doors, now appeared on the screen.

I must have fainted. When I came to, Jez, Max and my parents stood over me.

'Am I still alive?' I said more to myself than to the others.

'Of course, you are, but you frightened us to death,' Jez barked, the relief evident in his voice. 'I'm so sorry.' He hugged me tightly and wept.

I hugged him back tighter.

'You, you…stupid idiot,' my father grunted. I could tell he had also been crying. 'You'll never believe what we have been through tonight my boy.'

'I can imagine,' I muttered. 'Sorry Dad. Sorry Mam.'

The girl with the bandages on her wrists smiled at me knowingly.

Jez spoke again. 'I feel like I've been to Hell and back.'

I opened my hand; there in my sweaty palm was the ball from the roulette game. I kissed it. 'You have no idea; you have no bloody idea,' I replied, peering over again at the girl next to me. Then both of us burst into fits of laughter much to the confusion of everyone else in the room.

******

CLICK

The siren belching out from the speeding police car pierced the night sky. The vehicle raced up the High Street; lights flashing manically. In a matter of seconds, it disappeared out of sight.

Janie hardly even noticed all the commotion. Hand in hand, she skipped out of the restaurant with her new boyfriend on this wet but, for her, magical Tuesday night. The young couple sidestepped the puddles as they rushed through the soggy car park.

'That was a gorgeous meal!' Janie declared. Her voice was as bubbly as her mood. 'Thank you so much.'

She had only been going out with Darren for just over three weeks, but she already knew she was in love. He made her feel good inside, gave her goose pimples all over when he kissed her. On top of that, he was really cute, so good looking, and most importantly she felt like she could tell him anything. Anything at all. He was absolutely perfect.

They climbed into her father's car. The smell of alcohol from his breath soon filled every inch of the vehicle.

'Let's go up to the lake,' the boy grinned. He gently stroked her arm with his fingertips.

His touch made imaginary butterflies flutter in her stomach. 'I don't know … it's scary up there at night.' She wished she hadn't just said that. She didn't want him to think she was immature. After all he was used to going out with college girls. But her dad would kill her if he found out. She wasn't even supposed to be out with 'a boy like that'.

'How do you know what it's like up by the lake at night? I bet you've been up there with other boys!' he jokingly teased. She didn't sense the note of jealousy that had crept into his voice.

'No,' she said innocently. 'You know what I mean … it's just that it's getting late and…'

He turned away from her. Obviously upset, he tugged violently at his seat belt. Annoyed with herself, she drove out of the car park onto the main road.

'Take me home then,' he stared out of the passenger window.

Her heart sank. She didn't want to disappoint him. They were getting on so well, 'Ok,' she smiled, 'we'll go, but only for an hour … I need to get home before midnight.'

He clapped his hands. 'Great … let's stop and get some more beer,' he said, or rather demanded. He snaked his muscular arm around her shoulders.

She dithered. 'I don't know about that.' Another cop car overtook them, sirens blaring. She added, 'Haven't you had enough already?' During their meal he had drunk quite a bit.

'I've only had a couple of pints. Come on … it'll be fun. I know, I'll get you a coke or something,' he replied.

'I guess so,' she reluctantly agreed and pulled up in front of the convenience store. She watched him saunter towards the door. She admired his broad shoulders and his very, very cute behind.

Janie smiled to herself. She'd hated her new Saturday job at the coffee shop, until the day he had strolled in looking all handsome and cool in his white tee-shirt and jeans. She still couldn't believe he had actually asked her out. He could have his pick of anyone. He was twenty-one, tall, dark and gorgeous. All the popular girls in the town had the hots for him. Well, nearly all of the girls. Her friend, Kayla, had warned her that she'd heard he had been a real jerk to his last girlfriend.

'I heard he was often quite violent toward her. Gave her a black eye,' she'd told her.

Janie had heard a few stories, but she convinced herself it was just gossip. The girl was probably just jealous that he had dumped her, that's all. And to be honest, in the weeks since they had been courting, he had been nothing but a true gentleman to her.

Inside the shop, Darren searched the beer fridge for the strong stuff. He needed to think fast. Tonight, he had only one thing on his mind. His aim had been to get Janie drunk, or at least tipsy enough to loosen her up a bit. Deep down he knew she wasn't his type at all. She was really boring but she had a great body on her … a body that he'd been told by his mates had yet to be conquered. That was going to change. Tonight was going to be extra special. It hadn't helped that she had refused to even have a drop of alcohol during dinner at the restaurant. Now he would have to revert to plan B. He smirked to himself while paying for his six pack and her bottle of Diet Coke. He headed back to the car.

‘Pop the boot, Babe,’ he said smiling angelically. He blew her a kiss through the window. ‘I want to throw my jacket in, it’s soaking wet.’

She smiled at him, grateful for the show of affection. She opened the car boot and thought again how lucky she was. She checked her reflection in the rear-view mirror. She looked good even if she did say so herself.

Darren pretended to fiddle about in the trunk. He quickly looked around to make sure no one was watching. He unscrewed the top of the soft drink. He took a mouthful, spat it out and poured in the special liquid he had brought with him. He slammed the boot shut. Holding the beer and the coke, he slid into the passenger’s seat. He caught her staring at the outline of his muscular body through his damp shirt.

She noticed him, noticing her checking him out. ‘You’re all wet,’ she stuttered, her cheeks flaming red.

‘Don’t worry you can warm me up later … now, close your eyes and hold out your hand,’ he said playfully.

‘What?’

‘You heard me … come on, just do it!’

Eyes closed, she stretched out one arm, a nervous grin on her face. He placed a chocolate heart into the palm of her hand. 'Just for you,' he declared.

'You are so sweet.' Delighted at the sight of the tiny treat, she leaned over to kiss his cheek.

'... and, your Diet Coke!' He unscrewed the top and handed it to her.

She took a small sip. Making a face, she put the cap back on and set it in the cup holder. 'That tastes odd.'

'Must be the new flavour … they're always changing it.'

Outside, the sky was pitch-black. Heavy rain began to fall as they pulled away from the shop. The windshield wipers fought to keep up with the steady downpour that showed no sign of stopping. Janie clutched the steering wheel, white knuckled. She strained to see the road in front of her. She hated driving at night, especially in the rain.

'Do we have to go to the lake … the weather's terrible.'

'It's not far … come on … it will be so romantic up there in this weather. I'll protect you from the rain and the boogieman.' He gave her a dazzling smile.

Her heart did an excited, little jolt.

She changed up into fourth gear. She could barely see a thing in front of her. Carefully, she made her way onto the road leading away from the town and the stream of traffic. Another police car with lights flashing shot past them, going in the opposite direction.

'What the heck is going on tonight?' she asked, 'There's cops everywhere.' She fiddled with the dials on the radio tuning to the local news station.

Darren finished his first can. He threw it out of the window. He opened a second and closed his eyes. Inwardly, he felt kind of anxious but very excited. He knew as soon as the drugs kicked in it would be party time.

The woman on the radio spoke, *'... and the police say the man is very dangerous and shouldn't be app ...'*

'Haven't you got any music on here?' Darren reached over and turned the station over. He handed her the bottle of Coke, as Fall Out Boy blared from the speaker. 'Here, have another drop.'

She glanced briefly across at him. The tone of his voice had altered. It sounded a little threatening. She took another sip. 'This does taste really funny,' she commented, screwing up her face again.

'Let me taste it.' He pretended to drink it himself. He passed it back. 'Tastes fine to me. Come on, hurry up! Put your foot down.' He was growing more edgy and a hell of a lot hornier.

She took a big gulp before concentrating on driving.

He knew he had come across rather aggressively. He changed tactics. He leaned across to her and started nuzzling her neck. She moaned, finding it hard to focus. 'Stop it,' she giggled,

He continued to kiss her, becoming more forceful. The blood raced through his veins, the evil darkness waking up inside of him; his hardness growing in his pants.

'Stop it, I'm going to crash,' she giggled, feeling relaxed again.

Suddenly, without any warning she slammed her foot on the brakes. The tyres screeched. They slid on the wet tarmac. The car skidded to a shuddering halt on the other side of the road, facing the wrong way.

'What the hell did you do that for?' he cried, wiping the beer off his jeans. 'I just bought these bloody Levis … you could have fuckin' killed us … you stupid Bitch.'

'I saw someone.'

'You didn't.' He glared at her.

'I swear I saw someone standing in the middle of the road. He was dressed in white.' Her heart pounded in her chest. She looked apprehensively over her shoulder.

The rain slashed down on the windscreen, obscuring their view.

'Where?' Darren looked out of the window. 'There's no one there … come on, let's get out of here,' he snapped. He swore under his breath, while trying to dry his jeans against the car heater. His hard-on now drooping sadly in his pants.

Still shaking, Janie drove off.

Less than five minutes later they pulled into a parking spot near the boat ramp. It was a large, circular section cut into the forest with a view of the lake at one end. There were no other cars about. It was completely isolated. The large trees surrounding the area swayed in the wind. Janie looked at the hazy moonlight bouncing off the top of the water. The light shimmered as if it was dancing with the rain drops.

He reached across and squeezed her hand. 'Look, I'm sorry for shouting at you … really sorry! Come on, let's drink to us,' he said, motioning with his beer can and winking at her. They touched bottles and both of them took a big swig of their drinks.

Darren laid his seat back. He pulled her on top of him. He kissed her hard. She almost forgot all about her dad, and the trouble she knew she was going to be in when she got home. She let herself melt into Darren's embrace. As he kissed her and grabbed at her body, she started to feel lightheaded like some kind of mist was floating up inside her mind. She rubbed her eyes and reached across to try and wind the window down a little.

'Let's get in the back,' he whispered and lightly nibbled at her neck.

'I've got to get home.' She struggled to keep her eyes open. 'My dad's going to kill me.' She continued half-dazedly, 'I need some air … I've got to go.'

He tensed up abruptly. He pushed her off, his manhood wilting again. 'Not another daddy's little girl.' He took a big gulp of beer and turned the radio up loud.

The song drilled into her brain. 'I don't feel well, Darren.'

'Have another drink!' His words were harsh. His demanding tone echoed in her brain. She fought to clear her head.

'No … really, I've … I've … gotta get home. I've gotta get…' her words crawled out of her mouth.

‘Shut up and kiss me.’ He grabbed her face tightly. His other hand forcing its way up her shirt. He tugged at her bra.

Her body tensed up. She tried to pull away. She turned her face to the side, trying to avoid his sour, beer-tasting mouth. He kissed her neck hard, making his way down toward her breasts.

‘No Darren, not here … no, please.’

‘Come on … you know you want to.’

‘I do, but not here, and not now.’ She could see his features changing, and sense the frosty atmosphere. This was not the boy she'd thought she was in love with. She fought to push him away. She tried to struggle out of his grasp. It was no good; he was much too strong for her.

‘Leave me go … I’m going to be sick.’ She reached for the door handle. She screamed. ‘Darren, there’s someone there.’ She pointed to the clump of trees.

‘Shut up,’ hc placed her hand on his groin. ‘Go on rub it.’

‘No, honest … I saw someone … there.’ She blinked several times and wiped the glass.

‘Come on, baby.’

‘Darren … honest … there’s someone there.’

‘You'd better not be messing with me.’ He stopped what he was doing. He rolled the window down. He looked out. ‘There’s no one there you stupid cow … now stop making excuses and just enjoy it, because I’m going to.’ He knew the drugs had nearly taken hold of her. Soon he'd have her. He unbuttoned his shirt and pressed his body down hard on top of hers. He tried to kiss her again.

She pulled back, accidentally biting his lip. He slapped her across the face. ‘Bitch!’ He tasted blood on his tongue. ‘Wanna play rough, do you?’

She heard the smack reverberate in her head, but strangely enough felt nothing. Her head moved in slow motion, back and forth. A fog started to close in on her.

‘Not long now,’ he whispered in her ear, tracing her earlobe with his tongue. ‘You wait … I’ll show you who’s the boss.’

‘What?’ she slurred, trying to keep her eyes open.

The headlights from another car swung into the isolated car park. He jumped off her, looking into the rear-view mirror. The vehicle pulled up close. Its tyres crunching on the gravel as it stopped alongside their car.

A policeman got out.

'You better act cool,' Darren pinched her, 'and stay awake.'

The copper tapped on the window with his knuckle and gestured for her to roll it down. Groggily, she did what she was told.

'Everything ok?' He shone a flashlight into the car.

Darren dug his fingernails into the fleshy part of her thigh. 'Everything's fine officer,' he stuttered. 'We were just talking and you know … messing about a little.' His blunt, thick nails drew blood from Janie's leg.

'Are you sure you're ok, Miss?' The policeman stared at her.

She nodded, too afraid to speak. She found it hard to take in what was being said.

The policeman glared at Darren. He was just about to say something when he was interrupted by the police radio in his car. 'Officer Baton, there's been a sighting of the suspect near Gravel Road, over,' the voice blared from his device.

The policeman leaned into his vehicle and spoke into the radio. 'OK, I'll be there in five minutes, over.' He turned back to the couple in the car. 'I suggest you get home. Hear me … I don't want to see you here when I get back …understand?'

Darren nodded. 'Yes sir … we'll go, straight away.'

The policeman got back in his car, switched on his headlights and sped off.

'See what you nearly did?' Darren spat his anger at Janie.

Before she had a chance to reply his fist connected with the side of her head, sending her smashing into the window. He yelled obscenities at her. His words echoed around in her head as if someone was shouting through a loudspeaker. She couldn't move. She just felt numb and dazed. Darren leapt out of the passenger door. She could make out his footsteps on the gravel racing around to the driver's side. He opened her door and dragged her out by the hair. She was too drugged up to cry out. He threw her into the back seat and climbed on top of her. She struggled, but he was too powerful and she was too weak to kick, or scream. She lay on her back, staring up at the window. In her mind, she dreamt of being somewhere else. Somewhere safe and warm.

She could hear material ripping, rough hands gripping her body all over. She felt as though she was dreaming. Her body was like jelly, without substance or form. She felt powerless. None of her muscles worked. She rolled her head backwards. Through the haze of rain on the window she again saw a man's face looking down at her from outside the car. He stood there just staring, eyes wide open. No expression on his large face. Heavy raindrops streamed through his scraggy hair and on to his skin. Her eyes widened but she couldn't scream or tell Darren since he had one hand clamping down hard on her mouth, the other one shoved up her skirt. She looked at the boy on top of her and then back towards the window. But the face had gone.

Suddenly, she felt a sharp pain in her abdomen that took her breath away. Her mouth opened but nothing came out. Darren moved on top of her, biting her neck hard. He moaned and groaned. She wished she could pass out. The car rocked as the boy jerked faster and faster. Then the jerking stopped. He climbed off her, his breathing heavy. She lay there shocked and shaking. Her body all battered and used.

'Thanks for agreeing to do that,' Darren said arrogantly, He stepped out of the car and zipped up his jeans.

'You Bastard,' she muttered softly to herself.

He reached back in and grabbed her by the throat. 'Get yourself cleaned up Slut … before you take me home.' He snatched the keys out of the dashboard. 'I'm going for a smoke.' He locked the car doors behind him and walked into the wooded area, whistling with each step.

Janie lay flat on the back seat. She watched a fire fly circling around outside the window before flying off. She wished she could just fly away like that. It was extremely quiet, except for the rain dancing on the metal roof. She was too weak to sob, her body hurt. She curled her knees up to her chest and closed her eyes tightly instead. She drifted off to sleep.

Click.

A noise triggered something in her brain.

Click.

She opened her eyes.

Click.

She heard it again. She wondered what was making the sound.

Click.

Then she saw it. She saw the door locks moving up and down.

Click … opening … click … closing … click … opening … click … closing.

Click, click, click, it continued.

She lifted her head up, her insides throbbing with pain. She sat up. She couldn't see anything except for the darkness surrounding her.

It was quiet for several moments. All she could hear was the terrified beating of her heart.

Bang.

She screamed when the click turned into a solid thud.

Bang.

It came from the top of the car.

Bang.

This time harder, louder. It was as though the roof was about to cave in on her. She sobbed. She knew she didn't want him to touch her again. Janie looked around for some kind of weapon. She wanted to kill him. She couldn't find anything.

The lower part of her body hurt even more than the rest. A searing pain knifed through her. She curled into a ball, praying that she was just having a nightmare, and her mam would soon wake her up for school.

The sound of tyres crunching on the gravel caught her attention. 'Please let it be help,' she snuffled to herself. The car stopped suddenly at the edge of the car park. Janie's heart sank. She couldn't move. The banging on the roof became more erratic.

A beam of light shone through the windows. A few minutes later, another two cars arrived. Both did the same but at different points. Janie's car was surrounded.

'Miss,' someone spoke over a portable megaphone. 'Miss, you in the car … can you hear me?'

Janie placed her hands against the glass, followed by her frightened face. Her eyes trying to absorb what was in front of her.

'Good,' the policeman continued. 'When I say 'now', I want you to get out of the car and walk slowly towards me. But whatever you do, DON'T look back … understand? … just keep on walking, and *don't look behind you.'*

Nodding, she ran trembling fingers through her hair, and straightened her ripped clothes as best she could. She opened the car door. She could hear the click of the lock. This time she was the one who deactivated the lock herself. The headlights from the cop cars shone brightly into her face. Her legs were fragile. Her stomach ached badly.

'Walk towards me now … slowly … *very slowly.'*

As she made her way towards the officers, the banging noise got louder. She couldn't resist it. She spun back around to face the vehicle. She stopped dead in her tracks. What faced her should have shocked her to the core, but she had been through enough pain and suffering already tonight. Her features didn't alter when staring at the middle-aged man, in a white hospital gown, sitting crossed legged on top of the car in the pouring rain. He had something in his hands and he was banging the top of the car with it. He stopped and held it out for her.

'This way Miss,' the policeman pleaded.

Janie ignored the advice, and against her better judgement she drew slowly back towards the car with her arms outstretched.

'Shall I try and shoot him?' one of the junior officers said.

'No … hold fire … you may hit the girl.'

Janie stood next to the car staring up at the man on the roof.

'He hurt you … I didn't like that,' the man's voice was soft and tender. She looked at his hands. In one hand he held the car keys; in the other, the decapitated head of Darren. He then dropped both the keys and the head gently, into Janie's open hands.

'Thank you,' she smiled at him before turning around. She walked away from the headlights and towards the lake. As she slowly meandered to the water's edge, she was oblivious to the noise of the man on the roof of the car screaming feverishly at the top of his voice. She didn't see him jumping down and sprinting towards the woods. She didn't hear the deafening sound of gun fire. In her mind, everything was peaceful. She continued towards the water's edge, swinging Darren's head in her hand. She reached the freezing cold water. The police officers raced to ensure the psychopath, who had escaped from the mental asylum earlier that day, was actually dead before they went to see to the girl. When they finally got to the edge of the lake, Janie stood there singing to herself quietly. Darren's head was nowhere to be found.

Click.

She activated the car lock and laughed hysterically to herself.

Click.

Click.

Click.

******

SCOLLOP

When I was growing up in the 70's, there was one sentence that I dreaded more than any other as a 14-year-old kid, living in a crazy working-class house on a crazy working-class council estate in a crazy working-class town.

A town that made Beirut look like the village in Postman Pat.

And no, the sentence wasn't: - 'What have you been doing in that bathroom for this long, my boy?' or 'Why are your bed clothes as stiff as a poppadom?'

No, for me, it was, 'Jonny, nip up the shop and get me ten woodbine.'

Those ten words sent a shiver racing up and down my spine like a hotel lift being used by the local fat club on their way to Slimming World.

It wasn't because it meant me leaving my game of Subbuteo in my bedroom and running up the shop. In those days I was actually quite fit. I enjoyed sports. I ran long distance races for the school. And it wasn't the fact I thought my old man was smoking himself into an early grave. In the 70's everyone smoked; doctors, priests, dinnerladies, miners, teachers, kids as young as 8, women who worked in button factories, Starsky and Hutch and Kojak. In fact, all the TV detectives loved a cigarette…even Ironside liked nothing more than to lounge back in his wheelchair and puff on a cancer stick, or three.

No, the real reason I hated hearing that sentence was because the shops were a dangerous place to venture in those days, especially for a spotty, nervy, nerdy catholic boy like myself. Unawares to my mam (who would also then shout out from the kitchen, 'well, if you're going to the shops, can you pop into the fish shop and get us all fish and chips for our tea?) and my chimney smoking dad, the shops was where the Fish Shop gang hung out.

The Fish Shop gang were the cause of my anxiety. They were the Peaky Blinders of my day. The Galon Uchaf in-breds with more than a hint of the movie, Deliverance, and a dash of the Hills Have Eyes.

Their leader was a 15-year-old headcase called Speedy. Speedy would frighten a police horse in the dark. He was so ugly, the best way to describe him was that he looked like the last bulldog in the pet shop that had been in a car accident and had shot headfirst through the windscreen and then landed on a bowling green where the short-sighted caretaker ran over his beaten up face with the roller he used to squash the grass flat and then a piano fell on him from a passing aeroplane. You get the picture! He would have made James Cagney look like Johnny Depp.

The rest of the gang consisted of rats and weasels, who hid behind their vicious leader and encouraged him to beat boys like me up. I had never actually seen Speedy in action, but the rumours about him were endless. Tall tales about how he had beaten up a 28 year old karate black belt; how he had beaten up a tankful of SAS officers on a training exercise in the Brecon Beacons, and how he had pinched a lion from Bristol Zoo in his kitbag just for a laugh, and had let it go in WH Smiths in town where it had eaten twenty-eight women working on the tills and a postman who had gone in there to buy a pack of mints. I didn't believe the last one. The lion eating the women, not the postman buying the mints. Well, it would have been on the news, wouldn't it? I mean, the lion eating the women, not the postman buying the mints.

Anyway, back to the story, despite my fears, when my old man wanted his fags and my mother was sick of cooking, there was really no use me arguing with them, or pretending to faint, or play-acting that I was possessed by a demon. My dad needed his vice and there was no way he was going to go himself since he was glued to the tele watching the Wrestling on World of Sport. This was before Sky Plus and all the recording shenanigans. And my mother was too zoned out in the kitchen, high on downers and doing her weekly ironing. She didn't have the time, or the skills, to cook us anything.

Therefore, I planned my route as I always did. A quick dash up the lane to the garages, pop over Mrs Jones's fence, quick sprint across the car-park in front of the social club, then into the shop. Get the cigarettes; then, quickly duck and dive behind the parked cars, into the fish shop, get our tea, and run like the wind back home.

I mean, what could go wrong??

So, on that damp and dark Saturday afternoon, I completed the first bit of my mission. I got into Glyn's shop without being seen. The shopkeeper stared at me when I rushed in, nearly knocking over a stack of out-of-date baked beans. Now Glyn the robbing bastard shopkeeper (my dad's words not mine) was about seven-foot-tall, thin as Bobby Sands on his last day in prison, and the biggest crook since Pablo Escobar. He would sell his own grandmother's last good eye if he could make a fast buck.

'Ten woodbine please.' I asked.

When he turned around to reach for the fags, a quick thought flashed through my mind of, you know, maybe slipping a few blackjacks from the counter into my pockets. Lucky, I didn't, cos Glyn the robbing bastard shopkeeper (again my old man's words not mine) was a bit like the Child Catcher off Chitty, Chitty Bang, Bang. He could smell a stolen sweet from 600 yards. The previous Tuesday he had actually strip-searched a nun after he suspected her of half-inching a pack of spangles (and to be fair to him, she had pinched them).

I handed him the dosh before he would hand over the goods. With the fags safely stuffed in my pocket I poked my head out of the door. It was all clear. The Fish Shop gang who normally hung out on the wall outside the social club, like vultures waiting for a sick zebra to keel over so they could feast on its flesh and bones, were nowhere to be seen.

With my heart beating like a bird's wing I raced into the fish shop. Easy. I nervously grinned at Mister Fulgoni, the strait-laced, Italian chip shop owner who was almost fully round, almost fully bald, and smelt permanently of fried fish.

Sadly, for me, there was a lump of a woman in front of me, who had just ordered enough bags of chips to feed half of Texas (the state in America, not the shop on the ICI). I could have killed her. I waited and waited and waited until she placed the bags of chips in a wheelbarrow. 1 bag, 4 bags, 76 bags, 161 bags it went on and on and on.

'How many fuckin kids have you got?' I wanted to ask her.

The wheelbarrow was so heavy it buckled when she pushed it out of the door.

Then it was my turn.

'Can I have three bags of fish and chips and some scraps for the dog please, Mister Fulgoni?'

He knew I didn't have a dog, and I knew he knew I didn't have a dog, but I didn't care - I loved the scraps more than the fish and chips themselves.

‘Yes, yes, but I need to make a new batch of chips,’ he said in his Italian-accented, broken English.

I could hear the explosion of fat dancing as the sliced-up potatoes dived into the boiling hot liquid, like Kipper Jones showing off on the diving board up in Pant Baths.

I peeped out of the window. It was peaceful out there. I watched the clock hanging on the wall by the flipper machine. I slowly counted down the minutes. 10, 9, 8, 7, 6, 5, 4 …

I was going to make it. I was going to make it.

But then like three apparitions from the eighteenth century, Speedy and two of his slimy rats materialised on the wall of the social club. They sat there scowling into the big, front window of the chip shop. Since I was the only one in there, I knew they were gawking at me (well, two of them were. One of the rats had eyes so crossed he had to turn his head ninety degrees to actually see straight ahead!).

A shiver raced up my spine and booted me in the brain on seeing Speedy pointing at me while moving his finger across his throat like a one-eyed pirate on a ghost ship.

‘Oh fuck, trust that fat whale of a woman and her truck load of chips,’ I muttered a bit too loudly.

Luckily for me, the very religious Mister Fulgoni was lost in a world of frying and battering behind the counter and didn't hear me swearing.

Being a bit of a Catholic myself, I did what all proper Catholics had been taught to do in situations like these. I closed my eyes and said a little, silent prayer.

'Please God … don't let Speedy and his rats beat me up …. I will definitely go to church every Sunday from now on (a little bit of a lie), and I will go on Christmas Eve (a bigger bit of a lie). I will also stop swearing, and I will definitely visit my fuckin Nan more (a bigger, bigger lie), and, and, I will stop playing with myself … honest (the biggest lie since John Lennon whispered to Yoko that not only was she the most beautiful woman he had ever seen, but she was the most talented as well).

I hoped God couldn't see my fingers crossed behind my back.

I turned to face Mister Fulgoni. Maybe I could ask him if I could sneak out the back way? Or if he had any jobs going in the shop I could do, until Speedy got bored of waiting and went home for his tea? Or could he walk me home? I know it would be so embarrassing but I was desperate. But then I thought, what if Speedy beat Mister

Fulgoni up as well when he was protecting me and the chippy was shut down for a week? My life would be Hell. Gangs of housewives would be banging on my door with wheelbarrows demanding blood and bags of chips. My mother would have a fit, she often struggled to make four pieces of toast.

'There you are,' Mister Fulgoni said and handed me my order, wrapped in yesterday's newspaper. I pictured the headline plastered across tomorrow's rag: *'Boy shit his pants outside fish shop even before he was savagely beaten by Fish Shop gang.'*

I did the only thing I could do in the circumstances. I handed the fish and chips back, plus the fags and said, 'Mister Fulgoni, if I don't return in the next 5 minutes, could you deliver these to 17 Mitchell Crescent please, and tell my parents I loved them.' Then I added, 'Tell them whatever they do, do not look in my sock drawer.'

Without waiting for a reply, I spun around, took a deep breath and stared out at my aggressors. It was now or never.

Inch by inch, I opened the fish shop door. My hands were sweating. My bum squeaking like a children's toy.

Across the other side of the road, Speedy had taken his cheap jacket off, (which his mother had probably nicked from Liptons) and he was shadow boxing the lamp-post. His two rats egging him on like trainers getting a boxer ready for his world championship fight.

'Fuck …. why did my dad have to smoke? '

'Why didn't my mother make us proper food like, I don't know, tinned beef burgers and smash, instead of our weekly fish shop treat?

I shook violently as my right dap came down on the cracked pavement outside the shop. It felt like a scene from a cowboy film. Everything stopped. All I could hear was the chip fryer cooking the next batch of fries.

I stood outside the shop now. No safety net, no safety belt, no nothing.

There was a strange hush. No cars, no birds, no dogs barking. No drunks staggering out of the club and singing, *'Oh, Danny boy…the pipes, the pipes are calling.'*

We stood like two gunfighters, or if truth be told, one big ugly gunfighter and one very, very, very scared yellow-bellied chicken, squaring up to each other in an old-fashioned western movie.

Speedy growled and came bounding towards me, fists clenched and insanity in his eyes. His two rats followed behind him like grinning hyenas that had managed to sneak into a chicken coop.

Thoughts shot into my brain at 100mph.

Could I just run home and say I was mugged?

Could I pretend to have a fit and roll about on the floor?

Nah, that wouldn't work … I knew Speedy wouldn't care about that and would probably still boot me. Don't forget he had beaten up four hundred and fifty-eight SAS soldiers and pinched a lion … in a kit bag … then let it go in WH Smiths. He was crazy bonkers.

Then the nuttiest thought of all popped in my overactive brain.

I wonder what Noddy Holder would do if he was in this situation? I pictured the famous singer on Top of the Pops, wearing his big, glistening hat and his yellow-checked tie that touched the floor.

Why would I think that?

What use would that be for me?

Speedy was now only ten feet away from me. Then nine, eight, seven, shit, six, shit, five, shit, shit, four, shitty shitty bang bang … three … I could see his green teeth, and almost smell his stale breath.

Then bizarrely, I shouted out at the top of my lungs,

‘IT’SSSSSSS….CHRISTMASSSSSSSS.’

My advancing enemy stopped dead in his tracks. With a baffled expression on his ugly features, he looked around at his two side-kicks. They both shrugged. Then just as Speedy spun around to face me again, I booted him full-force in the balls.

BOOSH!

It was a beaut. The connection between dap and scrotum was like Bobby Charlton connecting with a ball at Old Trafford.

Back of the fuckin’ net…

He dropped like the ugliest oak tree being felled in the darkest forest. I could see the shock and pain in his evil eyes. Hands not clutched into fists anymore. Hands now cupped around his meat and two veg. He looked up at me like a puppy gazing at a family through the bars of a small cage in a pet rescue centre on Christmas Eve.

I thought ‘Well fuck me, I didn’t expect that.’

Then a bigger fuck me popped up. ‘Fuck me, what am I going to do now. I can't let him get back up.’

I regret what I did next, I really do, but at that time, adrenaline shot through my body faster than a Japanese bullet train. I booted him smack in the nose. It exploded, blood and snot covered his face and splashed over my right dap.

One of the rats leapt on my back.

I pulled him over my head in one movement. There was a sickening crack as his back connected with the kerb. I could hear the wind sail out of every inch of his body. The other rat looked at me as if I was King Kong who had just walked into the Wimpy looking to pick a fight with the chef. He turned and ran. His ratty tail firmly between his ratty legs

I actually felt like Clint Eastwood. I wished I had a cigar and a poncho thingy to fling over my shoulder. Years of sneaking up the shop, worried I was going to get battered took over my entire body. I booted Speedy in the guts about a million times, I do not exaggerate. He groaned each time. The rat started to crawl away. I booted him as well just for the craic.

'Get off, get off,' Speedy finally gasped.

I stopped; my whole body was shaking like my Aunty Joan's vibrator which I found under her bed when I was 6. Blood dripped from my mouth where I had bitten my lip in the excitement (not the excitement of finding my Aunty Joan's vibrator, I thought that was some strange device to stir cake mix with … no, the excitement of kicking the bully's head in)

Speedy and his rat got to their feet and hobbled away.

I felt ten feet tall.

I strolled back into the Fish Shop.

Mister Fulgoni held out my bag of food. He winked at me and handed me a scollop.

'Well done boy, this is for you.' He said, before disappearing into the back room to get some sausage rolls to place in the display cabinet.

I stepped out of the shop for the second time.

On this occasion, Speedy was slumped on the wall, trying to stop the flow of blood from his nose. He didn't look at me. Normally, I would have ran as soon as I got out of there, but today, I walked, no, I bounced like I was wearing the biggest pair of Doc Martens ever invented.

Halfway down my street, my best mate Thomas came running up to me.

'Dekka … Dekka …. you better watch out, I heard Speedy is going to batter you butt.' I smiled at him, 'Oh,' he continued, 'is that a scollop … giz a bite.'

'No way … I fought for this.' He looked at me confused. I bounded off into the sunset like John Wayne riding away from Boot Hill on Champion the Wonder Horse.

That night, the fish and chips and the scraps for my imaginary dog, were the best I had ever tasted.

****

BUZZIN'

Bongo stood perfectly still in front of the large, well-lit, blue-neon sign which flashed above the old crumbling archway. He took a deep breath. He swallowed hard on reading the three simple words displayed above the entrance.

'Welcome to Buzztown'.

Underneath, smaller letters stated that it was a weapon-free and friendly zone.

He used all of his many eyes to quickly scan his surroundings. He touched the lucky charm that dangled around his neck before slowly stepping into a section of the underworld he had never even considered visiting until tonight. This was where '*They*' hung out; this was where the flies lived. Here behind the large fish warehouse where piles of rotten carcasses of various shapes and sizes lay discarded amongst the boxes and cartons. He knew this wasn't a place for a teenage spider to be wandering around alone. In fact, this wasn't a place for a fully-grown tarantula who had been on steroids for two years to be wandering about alone.

'You must be out of your tiny spider mind,' his mate, Duggan the tailless rat had said to him.

Like all spiders, Bongo had been brought up to distrust other creepy-crawlies, insects and minibeasts. Earwigs, beetles, slugs, (he didn't mind snails) but it was the insects that buzzed around in the air that were especially hated by spiders. Flies were arrogant; they thought they had supremacy over all of the others, just because they had big eyes and could fly.

'Dirty, stinking bastards,' his granddad used to say. 'Eat the runny shit from a mad cow they would! '

His granddad never minced his words.

Yet, Bongo still found himself standing nervously outside the gates. Still waiting to take a deep breath and enter, but who could blame him? He wanted to see her again. He had met Greeneyez under Pier 14 during a heavy shower last Tuesday. He had been sitting there, between two pebbles, waiting for the storm to pass over when she'd approached him. Approached him as bold as a rebellious slug demanding extra salt on his chips. Bongo could hardly speak because she was the most beautiful creature, he had ever laid his four sets of eyes on. She didn't even seem fazed that he was from a different species. A species known for catching flies, usually making them into a nice, thick broth with a few mint leaves to garnish, plus the odd moth wing to mop the juice up with.

But underneath the old pier, the odd pair hit it off right away. They hung out all day in a dark corner, laughing and joking, hiding from prying or predatory eyes and, of course, seagulls. That was over a week ago and they had met up every day since. His close friends had warned him to be careful.

'Be careful Butt … 'em flies are nasty when they start,' Ashley, his best mate, hissed to him.

Naturally, he hadn't told his parents where he was going and who he was seeing. They would have never approved. They were old-school spiders. Insect-Arachnid relationships were forbidden; different breeds coupling up were bad enough, but different species? Unheard of!

He didn't care. At that moment in time, he was having fun; in fact, he was head over eight heels in love for the first time in his short life. Which was why he was standing here, a little nervously, in front of the entrance.

He took a sharp breath and quietly crept between the rows of bones covered in decaying fish flesh, looking for her house. The place stunk to high heaven. As he walked further into the fly-infested town, he felt hundreds of sets of coloured eyes staring at his every movement.

'What's he doing here?' someone hissed from way back in the shadows.

He knew the comment was aimed at him.

'Go back to your own kind … Spider-boy!' another fly shouted aggressively.

Bongo's heart beat like a drum in his chest. His legs, all eight of them, wobbled slightly, but he managed to keep moving.

An object, thrown from a chink in the wall, hit his shoulder. He turned around quickly. Nothing else stirred in the darkness. He considered turning back but decided to shuffle on, determined not to be intimidated. He checked the address on the piece of paper that Greeneyez had given to him.

He crawled into a long pipe, straight through it, and out the other end. Suddenly, a large bluebottle in a uniform flapped around next to him. Bongo stopped. He could tell it was a fly of authority. A Cop-fly.

'Lost are you boy?' the officer spat on the ground; his hand touched the baton attached by the side of his wing.

'No officer. I'm here to meet someone.' The cop-fly stared at him in disgust. The old officer detested spiders, even more than beetles … and he hated those almost as much as earwigs! It didn't help that his only brother had got entangled in a large spider's web when they were kids. By the time the young fly had returned with help, his brother was nowhere to be found.

'I'm meeting Greeneyez,' Bongo continued uneasily. He knew one wrong word could get him in deep trouble. 'I wonder if you know where she lives?'

The hairs on the back of the cop fly's neck stood on end. He was from the old school of insects. A school where flies bothered with flies, and spiders did whatever they did with their own kind. There was no mixing of species in his world. 'Spread them out son!' The officer pointed to the orange brick by Bongo's side.

'What?'

'You heard me, boy … spread them.' He pulled his baton out. His knuckles white with rage.

Bongo turned to face the cold stone. The cop-fly came up behind him and frisked him roughly. 'What's that?' he pulled something out of Bongo's pocket.

'That's my web-maker. All spiders carry them.'

'You ain't in Spiderville now, boy. This is a peaceful place, and that's classed as a dangerous weapon.'

'But…'

'There's no buts, boy, hand it over or … or else!'

Bongo could almost taste the menace in the words crawling out of the officer's mouth. He reluctantly handed his web-maker over.

'Now get on your way, boy, before I lock you up.' He spat at the spider's feet before flying away.

Bongo scurried on. At last, he found what he was looking for. He stood in front of the decaying remains of a huge monkfish. The surrounding garden area was covered in manure and other disgusting stuff. He felt sick. He stood there trying to build up enough courage to gently knock on the door, when he overheard yelling coming from inside.

'Get back in here now, my girl,' it was a male fly's voice. 'I've never heard of anything so stupid in my life … my daughter going out with … with … one of them!'

Bongo could see the father fly pacing back and forth in the window. He wore a white vest and was clutching a small brown beer bottle. He could also see her mother, bottle feeding seven maggots that wriggled about in her arms.

The spider stepped back to the side of the house, afraid to make a noise.

'I don't care, I'm going!' Greeneyez shouted back. She appeared on the front porch, slamming the door behind her.

Back inside, the sound of glass smashing filled the household, followed by a drunken cry, 'OK … OK … but don't come back.'

All the neighbour's curtains twitched as they strained to see what was going on. Bongo stepped out in front of Greeneyez.

'Hey … how are you?' he asked.

‘I’m OK … ish … thanks for coming. How long have you been standing here?’ She stared into his handsome face.

‘Not that long.’ He kicked a small stone on the ground.

‘I’m sorry you had to hear that.’ She appeared embarrassed.

‘Don’t worry … let’s go.’

The two teenagers walked back towards the archway. They passed by the prying eyes, with loose tongues, hiding in the shadows. ‘Spider lover,’ a voice grunted viciously from a second storey window.

‘Buzz off!’ Greeneyez spat back. She hated that flies were so small-minded. It made her ashamed to be one of them.

‘So … where are you taking me Incey Wincey … Spiderrrrrrr?’ she joked, unbothered by the ridicule that was being slung at them. ‘I hope it’s somewhere nice … I’m absolutely starving. I could eat the stinger off a yellow jacket.’

Bongo smiled at her. He loved the way she talked. He had never met anyone like her before. They strolled out of Buzztown, hand in leg, towards the centre of Tiger-moth Bay.

Several hours later, Bongo led Greeneyez back to her front door. The fish house lay in darkness.

‘Thanks for a great time,’ she laughed. ‘I’ve never been to a spider wrestling match before … it was quite an experience. Tomorrow, I’m going to take you somewhere very special.’

He grinned. ‘And where would that be?’

‘Wait and see.’ She kissed his cheek and then skipped up the stairs and through the front door.

Walking back home, Bongo felt as though he was floating on air. He headed back to the safety of his own part of town. His mind wandered in a field of happy thoughts as he walked through the dark warehouse.

He knew deep down that any kind of romance between a spider and a fly had little chance of being accepted in their society. It wasn’t fair, but then again lots of things that took place on the wild side of the docks weren’t fair. It was just the way it was.

Maybe they could run away, like his cousin Cecil, the money spider, who had apparently fallen in love and eloped with a centipede half his age. But Bongo didn’t want to just run off with Greeneyez. He wanted to treat her as his new girl-fly, and not the next meal for his many little brothers and sisters.

He grew more and more depressed at the thought of a future without her. He sulked his way back towards the neon sign.

Creeping around a large carton box, Bongo walked straight into the path of a waiting gang of teenage flies. He could sense they were looking for trouble. His black textured skin shimmered in contrast to the flies' lighter green, iridescent bodies. They carried weapons: bone splinters, glass, and pieces of razorblade.

'Hey Spider boy, who said you could come around here … messing with our women?' the thick-set leader stepped in his path.

Bongo bit his lip. He tried to manoeuvre around the fly and walk on.

'Go back to your own kind,' a smaller fly piped up. 'You eight-legged freak!'

The leader grabbed the spider's shoulder. 'Hey, I'm talking to you.'

Bongo reached for his weapon. 'Shit' he remembered the cop-fly confiscating it earlier that evening.

'Is this what you're looking for?' the leader sneered, and held up his web-making device.

'Where? How … did you get that?'

‘My dad gave it to me.’ The leader of the gang grinned. The others laughed.

Bongo didn’t have to be a brainy snail to realise he was in deep trouble. One on one, spider against fly, they all knew it would be no contest. But without his main weapon and facing eight of them, it was going to be tricky. Without thinking, he suddenly turned and legged it. He scurried in and out of the fish houses, around the boxes and other stuff that littered his escape. In hot pursuit, the posse followed. They were close behind him. Some chased on foot, while others flew overhead. They screamed and hollered. He ran and ran. His throat was dry. He was terrified. Panic took over.

They were on his tail. He bobbed and zigzagged in between the obstacles in a frenzied attempt to ditch his pursuers. He made a sharp left and ducked into a drainpipe, but he couldn’t shake them off. He sprinted out of the other end, but stopped abruptly, when he discovered he was standing at the edge of the dockside. Sadly, for him, it was a dead-end.

He was cornered by his hunters. He knew he only had two choices; stand and fight, or jump into the raging river below, which would mean certain death.

He turned to face them. The leader swaggered through the crowd. The razor blade glistened in the light of the moon. Bongo picked up a small piece of bone. His body shook all over. The two circled each other. The fly slashed at Bongo, several times, but each time he missed. He launched another attack but the spider was too fast. He smashed the fly in the face with his leg. The insect rocked backwards, dazed and hurt. Bongo looked to escape, but another fly cracked a stick down on his back. Bongo dropped down on three knees. Another blow took the wind from his body. He fell face down into the thick mud.

The rest of the gang pinned him to the ground. Blows rained down on him. He struggled but they overpowered him. He grew weaker. Another blow snapped one of his legs like a twig. He cried out in pain. With his eyes closed, his life flashed before him.

The leader of the mob pushed through the crowd and clambered on top of the spider. He turned Bongo around to face him, hatred etched on every line and contour of his face.

'Slice him Tommy,' someone said, handing him a small section of razorblade. 'Slice him good and proper!'

'Spider scum!' another yelled, kicking him hard in the side.

All of the fight slowly ebbed out of Bongo's body. His desperation now turned to grim acceptance. He stared up into the evil eyes of his pursuer. The razor blade inched closer to his face. Bongo touched his lucky charm. All of a sudden, his attacker somersaulted off him and flew straight into the water below.

Then another fly creature went flying through the air. There was mass panic amongst the remaining flies. Bongo clambered to his feet, wincing as the pain shot through his leg. He didn't know what was going on. The other flies flew off in all directions, buzzing in confusion. They collided with each other in their haste. Bongo picked up his weapon. He glanced around, unsure why they had given up. He looked upwards and saw two huge fingers and a thumb towering towards him. The finger then flicked another fly into the water below, before grasping the teenage spider in a gentle grip and lifting him up.

Bongo moved higher and higher upwards off the ground. He was afraid to look down. He then found himself staring into the face of a small boy. 'Dad, dad ... I've just saved this spider from getting beaten up by a gang of flies.'

The father shook his head while casting his fishing line into the river, ‘Look Dennis, I don’t care … we are supposed to be fishing … now come over here and watch where you put your feet.’

‘Can I keep him dad … please?’

‘No.’

‘Please.’

‘No, I said.’ The father sat down on his chair and checked his line bobbing in the river below the dockside, 'Your mother would have a bloody fit if you brought that thing in the house! '

The boy stared at Bongo for several moments, fascinated by the size of him.

‘You were lucky I saved you little fellow.’

‘Dennis come on!!’

The boy grinned at Bongo before flicking the poor insect high into the air. ‘Bye, bye Mister Spider … hope you can swim?’

The spider spun around and around, turning upside down before he landed in the cold waters of the furious river. He tried his best to swim but the current was way too strong for the teenage spider. He soon disappeared.

Next morning, Greeneyez awoke full of excitement. She decided she would take Bongo flying later that afternoon. He had told her he was afraid of heights but she couldn't wait to show him what the city looked like from up in the clouds. She waited as the sun came up and ambled its way across the blue sky. She stared out of her fish eye window, checking the time on the old clock near the harbour.

He'd said he would come around about one o'clock. He was always on time. She was getting really worried. It was already 2.30. She sat all day watching and waiting to see his handsome face appear at the end of the street.

The sun faded fast and the moon got into position. Greeneyez eventually changed into her nightgown. She closed the curtains in her room, a single teardrop rolled down her lovely face onto the floor. For some reason she just knew that she would never see Bongo her spider sweetheart ever again.

*****

FLOWERS

The leafy cul-de-sac lay deserted. The yellow, murky glow from the lamp-post gave it an eerie feel. Up above the moon poked its head nosily through the darkening, evening sky.

Two youths, suitably hooded-up for action, wandered menacingly through the lines of parked cars. Eyes shooting in every direction, hearts beating in their chests as loud as a drum solo.

Jac, the tallest of the two, had selected this street not only because Lakeside Gardens was regarded as the "well to do" part of town with plenty of rich pickings, but also because it was well sheltered and had lots of escape routes if things didn't go to plan.

'I can taste the money oozing from the houses,' he whispered, and licked his lips. It felt like a million miles away from the run-down council estate where he had been dragged up.

The teenagers carefully blended into the shadows.

'There!' Sully nudged Jac. They both smirked.

Within the blink of an eye, the side window of the green Ford Escort lay in a million pieces; Jac dived into the driver's seat, kicking-in the dashboard with his fake Timberland boots. He fiddled around with the wiring. Sully hopped into the passenger side, rummaging excitedly through the glove compartment.

As normal, Jac stayed calm. Super cool while his best mate skittled about like a nervous ball of energy. Giggling like a kid. Then Sully abruptly stopped. He stared at the magnetic statue of Jesus Christ positioned above the radio. The plastic, holy trinket gazed back at him. The boy made the sign of the cross before throwing it out of the window.

'Fuck you Santa.' He reached into his pocket and pulled out his lucky, little red ball. He squeezed it in the palm of his hand. 'Quick! Jac … quick … someone is coming!' the boy ensured his door was locked. He pulled his hoodie up further to cover his face.

'Two seconds Sul.' Jac smirked to himself. He loved the rush that "borrowing" cars gave him. Miles better than any orgasm he had ever had, even the one Mary Mullins had given him behind the skips in

Asda's parking lot; and just for the record, Mary Mullins gave the best blow-jobs in town.

Sully gasped loudly. An old man's face appeared by the passenger side window. 'Get out of the car.' He tried to open the door. 'Please get out.'

'Fuck me, it's Mister McGoo,' the boy slumped down into the seat.

Jac grinned. The guy really did look like the cartoon character. At that moment, the wires in Jac's hands sparked into life, followed by the sound of the engine kicking in.

Brrrmmmmmmm .... Brrrrmmmmmm. Sweet music to an experienced joyrider's ears.

'Yesssssssss.' Jac smiled at the man. Even though the rain was gently tap dancing on the windscreen, the boy casually placed a pair of sunglasses over his face. He shifted the metal beast into gear.

Sully resurfaced from his hide-out, stuck his middle finger up at the man and they were off.

Pirates of the asphalt road. Kings of the Wild Frontier.

Sully lit a cigarette, his hand trembling slightly. 'That was close.'

‘I told you not to worry,’ Jac moved effortlessly up the side road and spun the car onto High Street. ‘I would never let my best pal down.’

‘I wannna break freeeeeeee,’ Sully sang at the top of his voice.

All of a sudden, the same old man appeared directly in front of them, right in the middle of the road. His hand was outstretched. Sully screamed and covered his eyes. Jac swerved, but he didn’t have time to manoeuvre around him. The car travelled in a straight line. Jac slammed the brakes down, hard. The car skidded to a stop about twenty metres further on. An acrid smell of burning rubber filled the air. Sully clambered up through the sunroof.

There was silence, except for the rain that fell heavily now.

‘Did we hit him?’ Jac knew this would mean a long stretch, and not in some youth hostel, but prison. Proper prison.

Sully slid back down in the seat. His face lined with confusion. He shook his head slowly. ‘There’s no one there.’

‘What do you mean there’s no one there?’

‘He’s gone.’

The two friends looked back at the empty road, then at each other. Jac put his foot down hard again on the accelerator. The vehicle wheel-spun off towards the safety of the school fields.

'Get off me,' Jac cried when he was shoved into the cold, police interrogation cell. The door clanked shut loudly behind him. He stood there upright; his breathing heavy, fists clenched. He glanced around the room. It was completely white; even the table and two chairs. In the corner, near the two-way mirror, a padded table like a stretcher used in hospitals to transport patients about lay empty.

Jac had found himself in this situation many times before. He knew exactly how it worked. He banged on the glass. 'Let me out you Pigs … I know you're there. I can smell you!'

On the other side of the mirror, several giggles rose up.

'Concentrate, Jenkins!' a man's voice barked. 'Now, I want everyone to take notice … I'll be back soon.' A door closed behind him.

Back in the cell, Jac strolled over to the table. He tried to do his toughest walk; sauntering bow-legged like a gunslinger in an old cowboy movie. A pack of cigarettes rested on top of the table. He took one out, plonked himself down into the chair and swung his feet up on the desk. He searched his jacket pockets for a light. The old man appeared behind him. His smart, white suit matched the decor of the room.

'Do you want a light, Jac?' The man sat down opposite the startled boy.

'Jesus Christ … where did you come from?' Jac straightened up in his chair, and stared at the man inquisitively. He was sure he had met him somewhere before.

'There's no need to blaspheme, Jac,' the words crawling from his mouth were slow and deliberate. He offered the boy a light.

Jac leant forward, sucking in the smoke. 'Hey, nice suit buddy … does fuckin' John Travolta know you've borrowed it?' The boy snorted, amused by his own crap joke.

It was met with a wall of silence. The man's expression was as cold as stone. He stared at the youngster before casually checking the notes on his clipboard. 'Very humorous Jac … now, tell me what happened tonight with the car you stole?'

'I ain't telling you nothin' Porky.' Again, he chuckled at his own joke, but then straightened up in his seat 'Where's Sully? What have you done with Sully?' He cried out his friend's name several more times.

'I've done nothing with him … yet. He's over there.' The man pointed to the padded table. Sully lay on his back, throwing the red ball in the air.

'What the fuck?'

'Language, Jac,' the man chipped in.

Before Jac could say anything else, his mate lifted himself up like a teenage Frankenstein's monster on a slab, and waved at him with a big grin plastered over his ashen, white face. 'What a fuckin' chase Jac,' Sully added. 'You were like Michael Schumacher. Bastard brilliant you were.'

Pride spread across Jac's features. It soon disappeared upon seeing the serious look on the man's face.

'But Michael Schumacher … doesn't pinch other people's cars … does he?'

'Maybe he does on his day off,' Sully chipped in.

Jac laughed loudly again. The man glared at the boy on the gurney. Sully fell back sharply as though he had been violently pushed down. He went quiet, eyes open wide, staring up at the ceiling.

The man spoke, ‘Look Jac … I’m here to help you … you can trust me.' Jac shrugged his shoulders. The man continued ‘I can give you what you want, but first I need to find out why you did it.’ He reached into the desk drawer and pulled out a bottle of water. He unscrewed the top.

‘Damn Jac,’ Sully interrupted, ‘he’s a fuckin’ genie.’ He changed the tone of his voice to a much deeper note. ‘I’ll give you three wishes Master.’ His pitch raised up again. ‘Well, Mister Genie, I’ll have a cheeseburger, large fries and two million squid.’ He kicked his feet in the air.

‘This is no laughing matter.’ The man turned back around. ‘Jac. I’m waiting.’

Jac groaned, his knuckles white from gripping the arm of the chair. ‘Ask Sully first.’

‘I’m asking you, Jac. You are the ringleader, the one he follows.’

Sully put his hand up like a ten-year-old. ‘Oi, you, Mister McGoo! Jac’s the best … the best … he’s the Prince of the Stolen Escort … bbrrrrrmmmm.’

The man's voice boomed. 'I'm not talking to you … Mister Sullivan.'

Sully slumped back down on the bed again, motionless. Jac glared at the old man. He racked his brains to remember where their paths had crossed in the past. 'I don't know … I do it for a laugh,' Jac muttered. 'It's just something to do. Everything's boring otherwise.'

The man placed his fingers on his chin. 'Because you are bored … you ruin other people's lives … including your friend's over there.'

They both turned to see Sully in a world of his own, once more tossing the red ball in the air.

'What do you mean?' a hint of suspicion and anxiety crept into Jac's tone.

'Don't you remember?'

'Remember what?'

Sully piped up. 'Good God, Jac … he's a real nutcase. I think they've put us in a mental home by mistake.' He rocked back and forth. 'Help … I'm a joyrider, get me outta here!'

'Come over here Sul,' Jac motioned with his hands to his mate.

The youth on the trolley bed tried, but he couldn't move. He seemed to be stuck by some kind of invisible glue. A concerned look altered his usually happy expression.

'No … he stays where he is. Now, Jac.' The man tapped his fingers on the desktop.

Jac stubbed the end of his cigarette out on the wooden surface. 'You sound like my Old Man.'

'Well I'm not your Old Man.' The man slammed his fist down onto the desk. The teenagers gawked at each other.

'Least you have an Old Man,' the words escaped accidently out of Sully's mouth. The two glanced across at him. 'By the way, Mister McGoo … I know why I do it….why I steal cars.' The boy looked at the ceiling. In his imagination he was sitting behind the wheel of a sports car; the top down, the wind blowing through his hair as he raced along the open road. He gripped an invisible steering wheel firmly in his hands. His eyes bulged out of their sockets; a smile curled up his lips.

The old man asked politely, 'Why do you do it?'

'It's cos I wanna get out of this world …. I've been stuck in foster homes all my life, or stupid schools with their useless rules. I wanna drive in the Fires of Hell … that's it … I wanna drive through the Fires of Hell.' He finished his speech off with his own impression of Freddie Mercury. 'I wanna break freeeeeeeeeeeeee.' The tuneless melody ricocheted around the tiny cell.

Jac rubbed his eyes. He could see flames lapping at his mate's body, while little demons flew around the boy's head.

The old man broke the apparition. 'Well, that sounds reasonable Mister Sullivan. Let me see what I can do.' He turned around. 'Jac, it is your turn now.'

'What's this all about?' the youth asked.

'I told you … I need to know what you really want.'

'I'lllllll tell you what he wants … what he really really wants.' This time Sully mimicked one of the Spice Girls.

'Shut up!' the other two snapped back in his direction. He groaned and bounced the ball off the wall.

'I'm not sure,' Jac added, 'probably the same as him.' He reached across for another fag.

The old man moved the packet out of his reach and slid it into the drawer. 'But you are not the same as him … you are not from a broken home. You actually get good grades in school … when you bother to turn up.'

'You never told me that,' Sully stammered his words.

'Don't listen to him Sul.' Jac stood up and kicked out at the chair. It toppled onto the floor. 'I'm sick of this. Look copper, send me straight to Borstal … that's what I want.'

The man scribbled something on to a piece of paper. 'OK … straight to Borstal it is.'

Jac took his jacket off. He threw it onto the floor. 'No … wait,' he yelled, his heart beating wildly inside his chest. He sat back down, straddling the chair the wrong way.

Sully laughed. 'Hey … he had you then.'

'We're not talking to you,' Jac snapped back at his mate.

The boy brooded again.

'Who are you? What do you want from us?' It was Jac's turn to ask questions.

The man poured some water, but didn't drink it. 'Don't you know Jac?'

'Know what, for Christ's sake?'

'What did I tell you about using the Lord's name in vain, Jac?'

The two fixed each other with a long, uncompromising stare. Sully broke the silence. 'Maybe we should take him with us?'

Jac turned to his colleague. 'What?'

'Back to the car we nicked tonight …maybe you or him could figure out why you do it?'

'Don't be so stupid … how could he do that?' Jac mocked his friend.

'He can do anything … he's a fuckin' genie.'

The man pointed at the boy. 'You're not as dull as you look.'

Jac cackled at the man's observation, but soon stopped when he realised he was siding with the enemy.

Behind the two-way mirror, a loud gasp could be heard. 'He's not going to go with them … is he?' someone whispered.

'I think he is,' another voice replied.

In an instant, both joyriders were sitting in the stolen car. The old man sat jammed tightly in the back. He looked all out of proportion sitting there, clipboard on his lap. Jac drove. The tarmac road shot past extremely fast, the street lights mingled into one big blur. Sully turned the music up and lit a cigarette. He offered one to the old man.

‘No thank you.’

‘Go on … it won’t kill you.’

‘They may kill me …. but I know they won’t kill you,’ his words sounded cold, his stare was even colder. Sully shivered and quickly turned back around.

Jac concentrated on driving; his eyes fixed on the road. He was in the zone.

‘Faster Jac … faster … I wanna die young.’ Sully joked and banged the dashboard.

‘Do you really want to die young, Jac?’ The man touched the boy’s shoulder; his voice calm and devoid of emotion.

‘No!’ Jac drove straight through a red light. ‘Not when I’m driving. Driving makes me feel so alive. It makes me special … I’m not just a dumb kid from the wrong side of the tracks.’

The car swerved to miss an oncoming vehicle heading straight towards them. There was a loud blast of the horn from the other driver.

‘Get out of the way then, Grandma,’ Sully laughed.

‘So that’s it,’ the old man spoke again. ‘You don’t want to be a dumb kid from town … is that it?’

'Kind of.' Jac caught the man's glance in the rear-view mirror. 'I want my own set of wheels. I want to be able to drive anytime I want to. I wanna be the King of the Road. I want everyone to look at me when I go past.' He turned sharply into a side road.

Sully climbed up through the sunroof. 'Jac is the King of the Rooo..aa..d..d.' He pretended to shoot an elderly couple getting ready to cross the street.

In the back, the old man nodded to himself. He wrote something on the paper. Then, as quickly as they had found themselves in the stolen car, they were back in the cell, in exactly the same positions as before their little adventure. The boys looked around surprised.

'He is a genie, Jac, I told you!'

'So, are you going to give me what I want?' Jac said confidently.

'Maybe,' the old man replied, 'but first I need to make sure your mate gets what he desires.

'Fair enough.' Jac glanced across at his mate. A horrified scream escaped from his mouth. Sully was lying lifeless on the bench. His eyes open wide; fixed and glassy. Blood trickled down from a gaping wound on the side of Sully's head, pooling thickly on the floor. The red ball fell from his hand, and bounced several times on the hard concrete before rolling towards Jac's feet.

'What's wrong with him?' There was panic in the youth's voice. 'Sully … stop messing.'

The old man didn't answer. He pushed a button underneath the desk. A bell rang out in the corridor. Within a few seconds, a man wearing a white coat entered. He sauntered to the bench and unclipped the brakes on the trolley's wheels. Jac just stared, a look of disbelief on his face, as the porter covered Sully with a sheet and started to wheel him out.

'Where is he taking him … where?'

The old man wrote something else on the paper. Jac could make out the heading on the file. It had Sully's name on it in big, bold lettering. The man placed it in the drawer.

'He's off to see the Devil,' the porter sang, 'the wonderful Devil in Helllllllllllllllllllllllllllll.' He closed the door behind him.

Jac jumped up. 'I don't understand … why did you do that to Sully? He didn't do anything to you.'

The old man's face turned red with rage, the veins in the side of his head throbbed. His voice rose up several decibels. 'Why did I do it to him? It was you driving the car Jac … not me. It was you who tried to outrun the police car … don't you remember? I actually tried to stop you from taking the car in the first place!'

'What … what are you talking about?' the youth put his head in his hands. A sudden image flashed in his mind. The face of the old man banging on the passenger window when they were trying to get the car started. The same old man who stood upright in the road, just before the stolen car raced through the High Street. The images carried on playing, like an old movie on a projector screen. The car they were in ran the red light. Several cars swerved to miss them. Horns bellowed out. Sully yelled, turning the music up. The blue, flashing light from the police car appeared from the side street. Both boys sat snickering to one other. Sully gave them the two-finger salute. Adrenaline pumped through Jac's veins. He was in complete control. The car speedo touched 80 – 90 – 100 – 110. A worried look morphed across Sully's features.

'Slow down Jac … slow down.'

But the teenage driver just grinned, watching the coppers in the rear-view mirror. He careered into the new road, nearly losing control as the back end of the automobile skidded away. Jac readjusted the steering like a seasoned pro. He swerved to miss the on-coming bus, but didn't have time to pull it around the bend. Sully's cries were drowned out by the squealing tyres as the car spun around and around and smashed into the telephone pole. Sparks shot out from the body work.

Silence.

Jac opened his eyes; he could see himself lying in the wreckage. His body hurt badly. His legs were entangled amongst the crushed metal and the upholstery. He glanced to his right-hand side. Sully's face was bloodied; a cut on his head exposed half of his skull. Jac shook him; he felt cold. Then a section of his best friend's brains seeped down onto his shirt, like frogspawn floating on the top of a pond. Jac tried to scream but he couldn't. His throat was too dry. He heard voices and footsteps by the car window. People on their knees trying to open the door. Jac tried to crawl out the other way. He needed to get away. He didn't want to get caught. Then everything went black.

Next thing he remembered was getting pushed into the prison cell.

'Well Jac,' the old man's voice brought him back to the present. 'So, you did let your best friend down … didn't you?'

'I didn't mean to kill him … SULLY,' his yell sailed around the room. He kicked the door, banging his fists hopelessly against the metal. 'Sully … come back.' He held the red ball in his hand.

'It's decision time Jac. Do you want to join your friend?' The man gripped the pen firmly in his hand, ready to write. 'You can, you know … just say the word.'

Jac fell to his knees, his fists clenched. 'No … No … what's happening?'

The porter opened the door again, he stood waiting for his instructions. The old man walked towards the sobbing teenager.

'It's your crossroads in life, Jac.' The old man touched his shoulder. 'I told you I could help you.'

Jac buried his head into the old man's sleeve. 'I still don't understand … I don't understand.'

‘Have you heard the saying … if you live by the sword … you die by the sword?’ The man stared intently at the boy. Jac nodded. ‘Well, that car was your sword Jac … it’s time to pay the piper.’

The boy bawled. ‘Sorry … I’m sorry … I only ever wanted my own set of wheels; wheels that belonged to me … no one else. Please … I promise I will never nick a car ever again … honest to God … I don’t wanna die … I wanna go home … please … please.’

The old man turned and looked directly at the two-way mirror. He nodded at the porter. ‘Jac, I’ll see what I can do. Now, get your jacket and I’ll get Oliver here to help clean you up.’ The boy wiped his eyes and smiled weakly.

The old man strolled out of the door.

A minute later he entered the adjoining room. The muttering inside stopped instantly. The old man stood with his back to the two-way mirror. ‘Ok class … what was the moral of today’s lesson?’

All of the young Apprentice Angels sitting behind their school desks put their hands up. Their white wings twitched excitedly.

‘Apprentice Angel Jones,’ the old man pointed at the boy sitting in the front.

'Is it … You Always Get What You Deserve In Life, Archangel Gabriel?' the boy replied.

'Exactly, Jones!' He clapped his hands. 'Now, I want a twenty-thousand-word essay on my desk in the morning on, 'Why You Need To Be Careful What You Wish For.'

A girl Angel raised her hand. 'Archangel Gabriel … what's going to happen to Jac?'

Gabriel looked at the innocent faces lighting up the room. 'What do you think will happen to him?'

You will send him down to the Fires of Hell with his friend, Sir,' the girl replied.

Gabriel shook his head. More hands reached up to the sky. He pointed at a boy Angel slumped in his chair at the back

'You'll send him up to Heaven, sir?'

'Jenkins … have you been listening at all?'

All of the other Angel's giggled. Jenkins slumped down further.

Angel Jones spoke up again. 'You'll send him back to Earth … and … and give him a … a … car, sir?' his words were hesitant and lacked conviction.

‘Close Jones … very close … let’s see.’

Gabriel pressed a button. The two-way mirror turned into a large television screen. The Angels watched intently at a close-up image of Jac’s face. His eyes were closed. A woman’s hand came into shot and touched the young boy’s shoulder. He opened his eyes; they were red and puffy. He appeared to have been crying for ages.

The scene on the screen opened up wider. The youth was in a street. The young Angels in the audience gasped at the sight of Jac sitting in a wheelchair; his legs lifeless, his back broken. He held a bunch of flowers in his hand. He reached out and placed them at the side of a lamp-post. Other flowers and messages were littered around the base of the concrete post near the roundabout.

‘Bye Sully … sorry … so sorry.’ He fought against the urge to break down and cry.

His mother started to wheel Jac away. A Priest walked by.

‘That’s Archangel Gabriel,’ one of the Angels shouted out. The young, Apprentice Angels looked around for their mentor, the room was empty.

Back by the side of the road, Jac stared at the Priest. He thought he had seen the man somewhere before. The old man of the cloth bent down and handed the youth a red ball. 'Nice set of wheels Jac,' he whispered.

Jac stared into the face of the Priest. The boy pushed his mother's hands away from the chair and wheeled himself off into the distance. As he slowly moved along the pavement, everyone stopped and stared at the boy with his own set of permanent wheels.

******

NIGHTMARE

(On Evans Street)

Oct 08, 1980- something
Dear Diary,

What does it take to lose your virginity around here? I'm sure there must be something wrong with me and Rick. Neither of us seem to ever get lucky. Uncle Tommy says we couldn't score if we were millionaires wandering around in a downtown Bangkok massage parlour. He's one to talk. Aunt Marge isn't exactly a prize. The bearded lady I saw at the carnival when I was ten had less hair on her chin.

But I'm not that grotesque to look at; Ok I have glasses and a few zits here and there. On saying that, Todd Smith has got a lot more zits than me, and blackheads, and he's done it with girls loads of times (according to him). Is it that girls just don't fancy me, or am I not doing the right things?

And what good was that sex education class if I can't use any of it? What did the teacher say again? …oh yeah… "the man's penis goes erect and enters the woman's vagina"…aaaaaaahhh, that sounds too weird for words!!! Why did they have to remind me? They could have taught us something more practical like how to swim 100 yards in our pyjamas. Probably get more use out of that than the other thing.

I'm so depressed.

30th Oct
Dear Diary,

What's happening to me? I'm losing my mind. My hormones are raging out of control. I think they are the size of oranges and are racing around my body, eating up my sanity like a psychopathic sex starved Pac-man. I can't stop thinking of the opposite sex. They are everywhere I look. I can't even open the catalogue without it magically falling open on the lady's underwear page. Even my Aunt Doris from Newport, with the drawn-on eyebrows and the one tooth is starting to look attractive, and I find myself drooling over old Mrs.

Thomas when I'm taking her groceries out to her car for her. I'm turning into some testosterone filled werewolf.

Will this torture ever end?

Nov 5th
Dear Diary,

I need to control my urges. I need to control my urges … I need to control my … now where did my sister put that Victoria's Secret catalogue?

Nov 29th
Dear Diary,

I can't freakin' believe it! This is the worst day of my life. Rick is no longer the only other virgin in the class! It's just me now, Bishop Hedley's only pure, young soul. The only seventeen-year-old in Wales, no, the world, that hasn't popped his cherry. Not only did Rick, the lucky dog, catch a 2lb trout while on holiday, he also pegged his eighteen-year-old cousin's best friend in the cabin bathroom, while everyone else was outside roasting marshmallows under the light of the full moon. Flippin' great! Hope he has poison ivy!

I might as well just become a priest … or an astronaut.

Dec 3rd
Dear Diary,

Rick sucks! He thinks he is so cool since he banged that girl. He acts so mature. Won't even play paper football with me at lunch anymore. Says it's for kids. At this rate he is going to be older than my father by the time he is eighteen.

Dec 30th
Dear Diary,

Big New Year's Eve party tomorrow. Billy Day promised me there will be lots of booze, heavy music and hot, drunk, easy chicks to take advantage of. I hope so….

But what if I can't do it? What if I freeze? What if we get stuck together like those two stray dogs, I saw in the school yard once when I was in the year three? Took a bucket of cold water and several teachers to get them apart. How would I explain that to my parents? Or what if she turns out to be an alien from outer space and bites my old boy off? Being a seventeen-year-old virgin sucks, but not as much as being an eighteen-year-old virgin, so I hope Billy is right.

Dec 31st
Dear Diary,

Tonight's the night. I have two baths and a shower just in case. I put on my best underwear. Boxer briefs. I heard the girls in study hall saying they were the sexiest. No tighty whities for me. I've spent all afternoon squeezing the whiteheads on my forehead, and combing my hair over them so no one can tell. I can't wait. Wish me luck.

Jan 1st 2007
Oh my God Diary,

What have I done?

I don't know how to write this. I hope to God no one finds out. I'm still having flashbacks. Like the worst nightmare you can imagine. If that's what eight beers and God knows how many shots does to you, I will never drink again. The hangover was nothing compared to the aftermath.

I was at the party, minding my own business. Of course, Rick, the now hardened sex professional, was off in the corner with a group of non-virgins talking about the economic position of Venezuela and the effects of global warming, or something stupid and mature. They thought they were so cool; so intelligent. Like having sex with some geeky girls suddenly makes you a Sexual Know-It-All with an IQ of 159 all of a sudden.

I was there sitting on the couch, checking out all the opportunities. Sheila. She sits behind me in biology. That would be too weird. I can't sleep with a girl that dissected my frog for me. All I would be able to think about was that horrible smell of formaldehyde. Natalie. Now she's hot. Wouldn't mind that. She wouldn't give me the time of day though, and if she did her boyfriend would probably kick my ass. The last thing I remember was looking at Bethany's ass in those tight jeans before I must have passed out cold.

About 6 o'clock I woke up to the sound of a car alarm wailing off in the distance. My head was pounding. The whining noise entered the far corners of my dream and quickly took over it. I could only manage to pry open one of my eyes which closed immediately, as if operated on a very tense spring mechanism. I lay on my side facing a bright yellow coloured wall. My mouth was dry. I tried again to enter the land of nod, but something disturbed me. I didn't remember having a giant poster on my bedroom wall of Simon Le Bon from Duran Duran in a bathtub of champagne. I forced myself to open my one eye again to double check. Yes, it was definitely Simon Le Bon. My eyeball moved without the support of the rest of my head, and sent even more confusing images back to my sensitive brain.

The pictures sent back to my sleepy head from my second foray into the unknown reported that there was a bundle of women's dirty clothes sprawled all over the floor. On a dressing table, a million bottles of cheap perfume fought hand to hand combat with an army of empty cigarette packs. A disused container of baby oil lay exhausted on its side, fast asleep.

'Where am I?' I asked myself, too afraid to turn around and find out.

I could feel a presence next to me. I racked my brain for a clue.

Natalie? Sheila?

What day was it?

'New Year's Eve?' I muttered. No, it must be New Year's Day? I could see daylight poking through the broken blinds. My parents would probably be worried sick.

What happened after the party? How did I get here?

Although my subconscious knew the answer, it decided to just place its hands over its eyes and giggle wickedly.

'Roll over and see for yourself,' it taunted me.

I was too scared to face the music; afraid it would be a really bad tune. Like a bad 80's haircut.

Think! … House party, drink, someone smashed a table, lots of noise, people lounging about in the hot tub. Rick disappeared with some girl in a cat-suit. What happened next? Bethany. Great jeans. Great ass. Hangover kicking in with a vengeance. I didn't go with her, I know, but who?

'On fucking hell no!' I said out loud. 'Lois!'

I remember Lois, The Swallow, as she was better known, smiling at me from across the room. And just to clear something up before I go on, they don't call her Lois 'The Swallow' because she lives in a nest and flies South for the winter.

I remember her standing by the bar with artificial ringlets in her hair that made it appear like there were snakes dancing out of her head. I turned my glance away, back towards Bethany's ass, but her power of ultimate persuasion was too strong. I caught her advances full force in the back, which turned me around and instantly to stone as she welcomed me into her web.

'Not Lois, please God.' I felt like crying. 'Not the bald thirty-year old woman who worked in the Co-Op, and who thought she was twenty. Lois with the deep, husky voice and nicotine stained forearms?'

It wasn't the fact that Lois was completely smooth all over that frightened me so much. For as long as I could remember she had always been hairless. Some sort of alopecia disease had sentenced the poor girl to a lifetime of looking like Uncle Fester with pencilled on eyebrows. It was the little matter of her craving the company of young teenage boys that had worried me more. There was talk that she would demand that every boy she bedded bought her a cheap, twelve carat gold necklace, which she displayed around her neck. Often, she walked around town looking like Mr. T in a mini-skirt.

Suddenly, it all came flooding back to me. I recalled her dragging me home to her house on Evans Street, which is in an undesirable part of town and then, thankfully, the rest was a blur.

Had I actually had sex with her? I couldn't remember. I had no recollection, although it didn't look good. My body ached like I had just gone twelve rounds with Mike Tyson.

She cuddled in next to me and farted on my leg. A tornado of gas nearly burned a section of hair off my thigh. As the smell floated up and punched a hole in my senses, I felt like being sick.

I could feel eyes staring at me from somewhere in the room. I looked at Simon Le Bon. I was sure he was having a little chuckle at my expense.

'Go to hell you chubby 80's superstar.' I gestured back towards the direction of the poster.

I slowly looked towards the door and there standing in a giant-sized playpen were two small kids in white undershirts. They must have been between the ages of one to three. I couldn't help but notice that they had different coloured hair and skin complexions.

‘Why me?’ I asked myself. ‘Was I that desperate? Was I really that drunk?’ I continued to lie on my side cursing my luck and my lack of self-discipline.

Then I heard it!

‘Copy Mavis … copy Mavis.’

I sharply moved my head expecting to see a TV set blasting out in the corner, or one of the little brats playing with some new, Japanese wonder toy. But I couldn’t see any object that would have made those sorts of noises.

Then the words came again loud and clear. ‘Copy Mavis … copy … come in you stupid, lazy bitch.’

‘What the hell is going on?’ I muttered, pulling back the bedcovers.

I found no radio hiding there either, just the nakedness of her body and a half-eaten sausage roll.

‘I said copy Mavis … COPYYYY.’ The voice spoke again.

‘What do you want Fred?’ someone called Mavis finally answered. ‘I’m having a piss?’ The sound of water trickling filled the room, and played tricks with my mind.

‘Can you do a pick-up from Clark Road to the Hospital in about fifteen minutes, my petal?’

‘Of course, I can, Fred my dear’ she replied, flushing the toilet.

I put my ear to Lois’ stomach. I shot back in amazement on realising that the conversation between Fred and Mavis, who both ran a local taxi firm, was coming out of Lois’ belly, just above her special place.

Nausea took control of what was left of my sanity. I felt like running, but my legs had turned to jelly. I felt like screaming, but my tongue had hidden away behind my tonsils and refused to come out.

‘Oh no,’ my mind raced. Not only had I lost my virginity (I think) to an older woman with no hair and a gaggle of kids who would put the Children of the Damned to shame, but she also had the small matter of a talking abdomen.

Was she an alien? Had she bitten my willy off? I double checked. No, it was ok, but it did look rather red and worn-out. I jumped up and searched for my clothes. I had to escape. I stared at the kids who I now noticed were covered in Impetigo and yesterday’s Ready Brek.

'Should I take them with me?' I asked myself. 'What if they had talking belly buttons as well. Would they burst into song like some small version of Marie and Donny Osmond as I carried them into the police station.'

In panic, I frantically searched in the dim morning light for my trousers. I eventually found them still standing up in the corner of the room in obvious shock, with my underpants perfectly positioned inside. An image of Lois tearing off my Dockers with one tug of her expert hands, mouth drooling at me, flashed into my scrambled mind. I now remembered her pinning me to the bed and riding me to market as if I was a shire horse and she was on a mission.

I went all cold. I pulled my trousers on and buckled up the belt. I looked around for my shirt. I spied it on the floor, next to a three-day old dirty diaper. I raced towards it, heart beating uncontrollably. I placed my finger to my lips indicating to the staring kids to keep quiet.

Then I stepped on something very hairy and very, very scary on the floor.

'Uggggrh … what the fuckin' hell is that?' I pictured a rat with its fangs sinking into my exposed feet.

I kicked out at the hairy monster and stubbed my big toe on the side of the bed. Another cry escaped out of my lips. I fell to the floor, wishing that it would open and swallow me up whole.

I could hear Lois stirring on the bed. I lay there motionless, waiting to hear the unwelcome strains of 'Fee fi fo fum … I smell the cum of teenage boy!' departing from her possessed lips. Thankfully nothing came.

I crawled across the floor and tried to squeeze under the bed. I moved a cardboard box that was blocking my path. I recoiled back in horror on seeing a big, black face staring back at me with thick lips and an afro hair-do. On second inspection, I noticed that the face was made of rubber, and it had a bicycle repair patch on its neck. I checked the box that I had moved aside. There in large letters across the front it stated, *'Jungle Jim ... The best and most realistic inflatable man that money can buy.'*

'Oh my God! I've just been to bed with an alien who is two timing me with a rubber O.J Simpson,' I thought mortified. I would have laughed if it wasn't for the fact that this was a serious matter and my life was in grave danger.

I turned and started to crawl across the floor the opposite way. I bumped into a graveyard of discarded men's underpants, which seemed to have all but given up hope of ever meeting up with their once proud teenage owners ever again. I could envisage boys physically shaking as they ran, or staggered for their lives out of that bedroom of darkness: bruised, speechless and underwear-less.

I almost fainted when I heard the sound, I had been most dreading. I screamed when her head popped under the bed to face me.

'Hey you … what's all that noise?' she grunted.

'There's a rat the size of a tabby cat running around the floor,' I said rising up on my knees from the carpet. I was building up to the fact there was also an eight-foot six, rubber black man hiding in his box with a twelve-inch rubber cock.

'That's not a rat, that's only my wig darling,' a bald Lois said casually, then broke wind again.

She reached down and repositioned the artificial weave of goat's hair to her head then added 'and whcre the Hell are you going? We have some unfinished business.'

'You're possessed … you're evil.' I stood up. 'Strange voices … stomach … Fred … Mavis … what the Hell is going on?' I spurted out the words, pointing to her lower regions.

'Oh that.' She answered so matter of factly, while grabbing my hand and leading me back to bed. 'That's just my coil, darling. It always picks up CB's or radio airwaves.

'A what?'

'A coil. You know birth control. Had it implanted a few years ago when I was living in Birmingham.'

I glanced at the two kids.

'Ok. So, it doesn't always work but if I stand by the window, I can pick up the BBC radio 1 on a good day.' She seemed so proud.

She unlocked the kids from their cage and told them to go and have some cornflakes. She then threw me on the bed, took a bite from the sausage roll and grinned at me. I think I remember just before I fainted the song 'Save a Prayer' leaking out of her midriff.

I woke several hours later, Lois was asleep. I gave the kids some pop and let myself out.

So that was that, Diary. The worst night, and morning after of my short life. Lois had turned me from a boy into a man in the blink of an eyelash. The bruising and the hickies still haven't disappeared, and the image of Jungle Jim will probably live with me until the day that I die. I'm going to sleep with the light on tonight. By the way, I'm off tomorrow to buy a cheap, twelve carat gold necklace.

Jan 5th 2007
Dear Diary,

Finally told Rick all about it. He thinks it's great. I am now a real man. No more seventeen-year-old virgins in this town.

I'm not sure if real men are allowed to write in diaries …. think I'd better start watching football or reading the newspapers instead …

******

HOME

Harold sat slumped down in the threadbare old-fashioned armchair, in the shabby old-fashioned front room. A clock ticked away on the wall. The radio positioned on the sideboard in the corner belched out a Glenn Miller tune. The whiskey glass gripped in his hand had worked overtime that night, as it did most nights. Harold took another sip of the dark coloured liquid, and stared long and hard at the photograph of a much younger Harold, alongside his wife and a young boy sitting in the local park having a picnic.

The song on the radio got replaced by the news. Harold drifted into his own world when the newscaster told the listening audience how the virus had now spread across most of the world, and the doctors predicted it would get worse before it got better.

'... and finally,' the voice announced, *'remember, anyone over the age of 70, or suffering from underlying health conditions, should continue self-isolating until further notice. And now over to Sally with the weather update.'*

Harold glanced up at the ceiling. 'What?' he bellowed out, 'I can't hear you … hang on.' He turned down the volume. 'OK … OK … Beryl love … I'll be up in a minute, after I put the bin out ready for the morning.

Slightly drunk, the old man staggered a little on getting to his feet. He aimed towards the back door.

'Yes … I'll put my mask on.' He sighed to himself and began to unlock the five, heavy bolts that secured the door tightly.

1 … 2 … 3 … 4 … 5

Harold struggled to drag the wheelie bin up the uneven drive to the pavement. He looked up and down the dark street. It stood deserted. It had been like this, more or less, for weeks since the lockdown.

Harold, short of breath, pulled his angina pump from his cardigan pocket and inhaled deeply. After several breaths to clear his head, he teetered back to the house. He pulled the door closed but didn't lock it. He poured himself another drink.

'Yes … yes … I've taken my tablets, don't worry. No, I haven't been drinking.' He bellowed out, on gulping the whiskey down in one go. Unsteady on his feet, he switched off the front room light and clambered slowly up the stairs.

'Warm me up, darling, my feet are freezing,' he switched the bedroom light off and climbed under the covers.

From the shadows under the broken streetlight, Wayne watched the upstairs of the house plunge into darkness. He sucked the last drop of life out of his cigarette, flicked the nip onto the pavement and strolled menacingly towards the house.

'The idiot didn't lock the door,' he muttered to himself, 'drunken fool.'

He opened the back door quietly. Using the light from his mobile, he rummaged through the kitchen drawers.

'Fuckin' rubbish, fuckin' crap.' He turned around and accidentally kicked one of the empty whiskey bottles lying by the table. He held his breath in the silence. Nothing stirred. He checked the drawers in the front room. There wasn't anything worth nicking in there either.

'Waste of fuckin' time.' He headed for the back door, but stopped. 'I need something to sell … I need a score.' He twisted back around. He glanced at the stairs. 'Must be something worth nicking up there,' he muttered. He picked up a kitchen knife from the table and tip-toed in the direction of the staircase.

'What the fuck's that smell?' he held his nose in disgust.

Silently, he crept up the flight of wooden stairs, again using the light off his phone to show the way. At the top, the smell got worse, it was so bad he nearly retched. He opened the bedroom door. The light from the moon sneaked in through the curtains.

He spotted the jewellery case on the table. 'Jackpot,' he mouthed the words.

He snuck in and began rummaging through the drawers in the dark, still holding his nose with one hand. He turned to see someone lying in the bed, but facing away from him. Finding some money and jewellery, he placed them into his pocket. He opened more drawers. There were bits and bobs of decent stuff; an old watch, rings, more cash. The thief grinned. He didn't notice the shadow of the old man creeping up behind him, clutching a bedpan.

The youth suddenly heard the sound of someone breathing heavily right behind him. Wayne swung around; his mobile phone lit up Harold's twisted face.

BANG!

Darkness.

When Wayne opened his eyes several minutes later, he found himself tied to a chair in the bedroom, with the moth-eaten cord of a dressing gown. Blood from a head wound dribbled down into his mouth.

'Oh look, he's awake.' Harold walked over to him. He spat on a hanky and started to wipe the blood away from the boy's mouth. The old man pushed his face right up to the teenage boy, and smiled softly. He then turned to peer into the corner, where the other person still lay in the bed with their back to them. 'I'm sorry Beryl … I know I shouldn't have hit him, but I thought he was a burglar.' He continued to wipe away the blood from Wayne's face. 'But he's fine now … look … he's sitting up in the chair.'

Harold smoothed the young boy's hair. He thrust his hand into Wayne's pocket and took back the jewellery and money. He placed them regimentally back into the drawers.

'What the hell are you doing, sir? Let me go... let me go.' Wayne wriggled in the chair. Behind him, Harold picked up a can of fly spray and squirted it liberally around the room.'Oi ... I'm talking to you ... let me go you crazy bast...ard ...'

Harold turned sharply, the spray can still in his hand 'What have I told you about cursing in front of your mother?'

'What?'

'You know what ... no swearing ... your mother doesn't like it.'

'What the fuc...' The old man glared at him again. Wayne quickly added, 'What are you talking about?'

Harold ignored him. 'Yes, love ... he's still got that old, cheeky grin.' He pinched the boy's cheek playfully and smiled.

'Get off me.'

'I know ... I'll make us all a nice cup of tea. would you like that son?' He turned to the bed. 'Yes ... yes ... of course love ... I'll make it in his special mug. I remember. Yes ... and I'll bring the biscuits.'

He rolled his eyes at Wayne. 'She worries about you, see? … always has.' Harold ambled out of the room and shuffled downstairs.

After a few seconds, Wayne wriggled and twisted, trying with all his might to break free of the tightly knotted cord. It was no use - the bloke must've been a boy scout back in the day! He tried to bend around to see the woman. He could hear the tap running down in the kitchen, then the click of the kettle's switch. The boy tried desperately to get out of the chair.

'Hey, Missus … quick, untie me … quick, please, let me go. I'm sorry I broke in … I am … honest.'

His plea was met with a deathly silence. Flies buzzed about the room. Wayne's blood ran cold on hearing Harold locking the back door. Wayne counted each bolt being locked.

'1 … 2 … 3 … 4 … 5. He's locked the back door … he's locked the back door … fuckin' hell … five bolts…five bolts.'

Panic set in.

Turning his chair slightly, he saw the kitchen knife positioned on the edge of the bed. As quietly as he could, he inched closer to the bedstead. He twisted the chair around and tried to grab the knife with his tied hands. Wayne stretched and stretched; his hand touched the knife handle. He reached across a little more. The old, wooden chair he was on toppled over sending the youth crashing to the floor. As he fell, his hand accidently pulled the blanket off the bed.

'What the fuck?' From the floor, he stared up at several pillows where the woman was supposed to be. 'She's pillows … pillows.'

Harold entered the room with the tray of tea. Calmly he placed it on the sideboard and lifted the boy up. He slid the chair back to the other side of the room, and picked the knife back up off the floor.

'Been catching up on old times have you?' Wayne began to physically shake with fear. Harold continued, 'Beryl love … you've kicked your blanket off again have you? Let's get you nice and comfortable, is it?' He propped 'her' up in bed and turned back to the boy. 'She's always doing that … nightmares she says. Eating too much cheese before bedtime, I say … she loves cheese on toast see … but you know that already, don't you son?'

Harold took one of the mugs of tea to his 'wife' and left it on the bedside cabinet. He placed a Kit-Kat next to the mug, then pulled up a small stool next to Wayne. He pulled a second Kit-Kat bar from out of his pocket and ran his finger down the foil, splitting it in two. He snapped the chocolate bar in half.

'There's just something about the noise a Kit-Kat makes when you snap it in half.' The smile on his face grew wider. He turned back to face the bed. 'We love Kit-Kats don't we, love? … especially on special occasions … and this is a very, very special occasion.' He offered the boy half of the chocolate bar. Wayne shook his head. Harold carefully tucked the snack inside the boy's pocket. 'Keep it for later, but don't tell her,' he whispered.

Wayne started to cry. 'Let me go … please, Mister.'

Again, the old man ignored him. 'We've been waiting for you to come back … we've left your room exactly as it was.'

'What are you talking about? I've never seen you before in my life.'

Harold sipped his tea. He walked over to the sideboard and picked up an old biscuit tin. 'I know, let's have a look at some old photos of us.'

'I don't know what you are talking about.'

'Don't worry, Beryl, love, it must have been that bump on the head he had.' Harold held a photo up to Wayne's face. 'Look … that's me and your mother on our wedding day. Yes, it is me in my army uniform.' He stood up straight to attention, and saluted. 'Butler

876765, Sir.' Turned to the bed. 'Yes, I know! I was a handsome bugger.' He walked across and kissed the pillow. 'And you look as stunning today as you did way back then, love.'

Behind his back, Wayne grappled with the cord wrapped around his hands.

Harold showed him more photos. 'This is just after your mother had you … seven pounds, three ounces you were. The nurse said you were the best baby they'd ever had there.' He showed him another. 'That's one of us playing football in the park … you were four then … like a little Georgie Best you were. And this was me and your mother after you …,' his voice dropped a few notches, 'after you … you.' He stared off into the distance.

Wayne looked at the old man standing there. Harold turned to his wife. 'What Beryl, love? Your tea is too hot … OK … let me blow on it for you.' He picked the mug up and softly blew on the liquid.

'This is messed up, Mister, you need help,' Wayne muttered, 'I swear you need help … let me go … please.'

'But we've been waiting for you to come back, son.'

'I've never seen you before.'

Harold ignored him again. Instead he just sipped on his tea. The boy glanced around the room, trying to see if he could pick out a trace of sanity in all of the madness.

'Drink your tea, dear while it's nice and hot … OK … OK … I'll tell him … I will.'

Wayne stared at 'both' of them in turn. Snot ran down his nose, into his mouth.

'Your mother said you are so handsome.' He stroked the side of his face, 'and you are Jonathan … you've grown into a fine young man.'

'Who's Jonathan? What's going on?'

Harold wiped the boy's face with a small tea towel. 'I knew you'd come back to us. I knew.' He turned to the bed, his voice raised up another few notches, 'I told you Beryl … didn't I. What did you say?' He limped back over to the bed. 'I said I would look after him this time. It wasn't my fault. It wasn't.' He looked at Wayne. 'You believe me, don't you son?'

'What are you on about?'

'It must be the crash, love. He did hit his head hard. He'll remember us soon.'

'W… w…. w… what fuckin' crash?'

'Jonathan … language!' Harold turned to face the bed again. 'Shut up Beryl … don't start … stop going on and on and on … like a broken record. Shut up … shut up.' He slammed his cup down. Tea spilled over the bed covers. 'Tell her Jonathan … tell your mother.' He grabbed the boy's face to look at him. 'Go on … tell her.'

'I'm … I'm not Jonathan … I'm Wayne … Wayne Harris.'

The old man pointed to where his 'wife' was lying in the bed. 'It's you, it is Beryl … you never forgave me … never ever.' He put his arm around the boy. 'Look son … I'm sorry … I screwed up. I won't make the same mistake again… never … you believe me, don't you … shut up Beryl.' He put his head in his hands. 'I'm warning you. one more word … and you will be in the cupboard, with the other one … understand! Now, tell her Jonathan, tell her!'

Wayne looked at the cupboard in the corner, the door was shut tight. 'Forgive you for what? For what sir?'

Harold stood over the bed covers. 'It's you … you never forgave me … never.' He marched over to the boy and dropped down on his knees in front of him. 'Look son … I'm sorry … I screwed up. I won't make the same mistake again … never… you believe me don't you … shut up Beryl … I'm warning you.'

'I don't understand … forgive you for what?'

Harold stared out of the netcurtains. 'One drink I had … ok, maybe two or three … but I wasn't drunk. Far from it.'

He moved the small stool in front of Wayne's chair, like he was driving a car.

'I'd only had a few … we were only going 500 yards, but it was raining.' As he turned to face Wayne, his voice changed, like he was telling a small boy to behave himself. '... and don't forget, son, we've been to the park … we haven't been in the pub … ok?'

Still perching on the stool, Harold pretended to start up a car. 'I should have strapped you in … but it was late, we needed to get home. We were only going a few streets … only a few streets.' He looked back over his shoulder, 'Jonathan … Jonathan stop messing with that yo-yo.'

'What?' Wayne said.

Harold turned back around. 'I only took my eyes off the road for a second, only a second. I didn't see the other car.'

BANG

CRASH

Harold made the noises and played out the actions of a car crash. Silence. He picked his head up from the invisible steering wheel.

'I should have strapped you in … shouldn't have drunk that last pint … shouldn't have done this, shouldn't have done that … we were only driving 500 yards … 500 yards!' Harold got up from the stool. He reached down as if he was picking the body of a small child up from the ground. He carried it past Wayne and gently placed it into an imaginary box, sliding it under the bed. 'It was the other driver's fault. He pulled out on us … not mine … I couldn't let her see what I had done.' Harold looked at Wayne, a genuine sadness on his face.

Wayne could hear his own heart beating hard in his chest.

The old man's voice changed, becoming more aggressive. 'I know I should have left the car at the pub and walked home … but I didn't … I didn't … ok.' Harold closed his eyes and started breathing heavily. A weird looking smirk covered his face. 'But he's back now … look, no harm done.'

Wayne again fought to break free. Harold snapped back into life. 'Jonathan … you haven't touched your tea.'

'I'm not Jonathan. You ain't my parents. My father's in prison … my mother works in the betting shop in town … we live up on the estate. I wanna go home.'

'Your tea's getting cold, son.' The old man stood beside the boy. He picked the mug up. 'Just one sip … and everything will be alright … just like the old days.' Harold forced himself to take a few sips. 'Three sugars … just the way you like it. Good boy. I know … let's take your picture. We haven't taken one for ages.

'What?'

The man rummaged around in a drawer near the door. He pulled out an old polaroid camera.'We haven't used this since … since … well you know.' He stood in front of Wayne. 'Smile then Jonathan … show us that lovely smile of yours.' Wayne looked sideward, shaking his head in defiance. 'Smile, I said … fuckin' smile.' He snapped back towards the bed. 'I'm sorry … but he wouldn't listen … he's got your way about him … stubborn. Oh, don't start … yeah … if it wasn't for me, he wouldn't be here now, would he?'

He held up the camera, until the boy smiled. He took the photo. He shook the negative in his hand waiting for the photograph to develop. 'Lovely.' He cut out the boy's face and stuck it in the photo of the old couple using sticky tape. He showed his imaginary wife and whispered in her ear. ‘OK … I'll tell him. Jonathan … your mother asked if you would like to sleep in here with us tonight … she's even got your old pyjamas.’

‘I'm not your son … I'm not … please believe me … let me go.’ Wayne's mouth was so dry he could hardly get his words out.

‘Yes, Beryl … he's still in shock. Now dear, let's get you settled down again … you need your beauty sleep.’ He started to tuck the ‘woman’ in.

In a state of desperation, a thought popped into Wayne's head. ‘Mam … dad,’ he muttered. The old man spun to face him. Wayne smiled. ‘Mam … dad … I've missed you so much.

‘Jonathan … Jonathan.’ Harold made a face at the pillows. ‘I told you he'd come back … didn't I?’

‘Dad … it wasn't your fault, you weren't drunk … it was the other driver … it was … untie me, dad … I want to cwtch you both up.’

‘I told you, Beryl … it wasn't my fault … even Jonathan said it.’ The man untied him. ‘I told you.’

Once free, Wayne jumped up, pushing Harold to the floor. 'You sick bastard … you sick motherfucker.' In temper, the youth smashed the ornaments off the sideboard.

'Jonathan … don't …'

'Are you crazy? Mental-case.'

'Son!'

'I'm not your fuckin' son.'

'Jonathan … stop … you're upsetting your mother.' Harold cowered on the ground, near the bed.

'She's not my mother. It's a pillow … a fuckin' pillow.' He rushed to the bed and snatched up one of the pillows. He threw it at the old man.

'Jonathan … why are you acting like this?'

'I'm not acting you fuckin' weirdo.'

'But son, I love you.' He picked up the pillow and held it up by his face. 'We both love you.'

Wayne shouted. 'I'm not your son … how many times have I got to tell you. Fuck knows where he is.' He stopped talking and looked at the bed. 'Hang on …'

'Don't son … don't.'

On one knee, Wayne's eyes scanned the space beneath the bed. He reached under and pulled out a large box. He slowly opened the lid. ‘Arrrrrrgggggghhhh … fucking hell … what have you done?’ He looked at the small skeleton bones in the box and dropped it to the floor with a clatter.

‘Don’t upset your mother son … she hasn’t been very well.’

‘Hasn’t been fucking well … are you joking?’

‘Quiet, son.’

‘Where is she …?

Harold glanced at the cupboard. Wayne followed his stare.

‘Shut up, you said to her … shut up or I’ll put you in the … in the … cupboard … with the other one.’

The youth walked over to the cabinet. He took a deep breath then pulled open the door. He screamed and recoiled backwards almost tripping over. He started to dry heave. ‘Fuckin' hell … fuckin' hell. She’s dead … and so is your son.’

He kicked the box with the bones in it across the room.

‘Did you kill her as well?’

‘Shut up.’

‘You did … didn’t you?’

'She won't shut up about it … about you … blaming me … all the time … it wasn't my fault … I told her … but she wouldn't let it go … on and on and on … day after day after day … I couldn't breathe anymore.' The man clutched at his heart. He pulled out the angina pump from his pocket. Wayne snatched it out of his hand.

'Oh no you don't … I've got a few questions… beat her to death, did you? Or strangled her when she slept. Murderer … I'm going to the police.' Wayne's eyes felt heavy. He began to feel funny, dizzy. He shook his head. Harold picked the bones up off the floor and put them back in the box. He grinned at the boy.

Wayne wobbled backwards bumping into the wall. 'What's happening?'

Harold clambered up onto his feet. 'If you must know I put a few drops of thiopental sodium in her teeeeea.'

'What?'

'Poison … like rat poison … but quicker … in her favourite mug as well.'

Wayne shot a glance at the mug the old man had made him drink out of. He dropped the pump on the ground while reaching out to steady himself. 'Have you done it to me?'

Harold opened up his arms. 'Don't fight it son.'

The boy started to choke, he strained to breathe properly. 'What have you done to me?' The boy tried to throw a punch, but he was too weak. He stumbled out of the room, across the hallway. Harold followed behind, holding the batman mug. Wayne almost fell into a second bedroom. Over the small, single bed hung a sign:

'Welcome Home Jonathan'. Wayne collapsed on the bed. Harold followed him in. He stroked the boy's face.

'Welcome home son. We have missed you so much.' He lifted the boy's feet up onto the bed and tucked him in. 'Now let's all promise that we will never leave each other again.'

The old man picked up the batman mug and swallowed a big mouthful of tea. He turned on a kid's mobile toy that dangled above them. The tune from the mobile played softly.

'Night, night everyone.' Harold closed his eyes.

******

PROMISE

Joe rushed through the main doors of the General Hospital, nearly stumbling over on the newly polished floor by reception. He looked about for directions. His head was spinning too much for him to take anything in.

He stopped a nurse. 'Can you tell me where the intensive care ward is please?'

She pointed straight ahead and gave him the 'don't worry, it will be ok' kinda smile that nurse's always do. He almost sprinted through the corridor, passing the shop selling newspapers and chocolate; passing the lifts and a woman getting wheeled into X-ray by a porter with headphones in his ears. He saw the sign for intensive care. Another nurse pointed him to a private room at the end of the strangely peaceful ward.

Joe stopped by the door to the room. Part of him was afraid to open it. He really didn't want to see what it was that awaited him on the other side. He took a deep breath, knocked quietly and entered. It was like a scene from a poorly written hospital TV show. A man in a white coat, who he assumed was a doctor stood near a bed scribbling notes on a chart. The life support machine bleeped in the corner of the room like one of those old computerized table tennis games.

'How is he doc?' Joe stared at his father lying unconscious in the bed.

'I'm afraid he's had a massive stroke.'

Joe slumped down in the chair next to the bed. He felt as though someone had punched him full-force in the stomach. He struggled to gain his breath. He squeezed his old man's hand. It felt warm.

The doctor added, 'He's more stable now … but … but….'

'But what, Doc?'

'It's very unlikely he'll be able to walk or even talk again … he will probably be paralysed for the rest of his life.'

Joe placed his head in his hands. As if the imaginary punch to the guts wasn't bad enough, the doctor's last sentence felt like a boot in the nuts off someone wearing steel toe-capped docs.

The doctor headed for the door 'I know it's tough … but at least you can be thankful that he's still alive.'

'Can I?' Joe muttered.

The doctor departed. Joe stared at his father's face. He looked so peaceful lying there. As though he was just taking a nap on his favourite chair next to the fire, tv remote resting on the arm, slippers on his feet.

Joe punched the bed. 'Why dad? Why did you make me do it? Why? That's not fair, not fair … you … you're … going to ruin my life … our lives.'

He remembered that day in the park two years before. Joe's two small sons, Daniel and Scott, climbing up the steps to get to the top of the slide. Joe and his old man, Ronny sat on a park bench watching their progress. It was a blisteringly hot day. The park was packed more than usual with screaming kids and gossiping mothers.

'Look at us gramp,' Daniel shouted down from near the top, waiting for their turn to go.

Ronny waved at them as the two brothers slid down together. Ronny turned back to his own son. He held out his hand. Joe looked at it with uncertainty. His dad was never the type of father that did emotion well. He loved him but he never hugged him like Joe hugged his own children. But fathers of that generation rarely did.

'Ok, son … is it a deal?' Ronny asked.

'Don't be stupid dad.'

'Don't speak to your old man like that … I'm far from stupid … now shake on it.'

Joe reluctantly took his father's hand in his and they shook.

'You can never break your promise, son … don't forget … it's important to me … ok?'

Joe looked his father in the eyes. They stared at each other for twenty long seconds. 'OK … dad … I won't break my promise.'

A nurse entering the hospital room, snapped Joe out of his daydream.

'Would you like a cup of tea?' she asked.

'No,' Joe replied, 'I've got to go home to tell the family.'

Forty minutes later, Joe opened the front door to his three-bedroom house on the new estate at the edge of the town. His two, small boys came running towards him. His wife, Helen, stood in the kitchen doorway; a glass of white wine in her hand. Her eyes puffed up from the crying.

'How's gramper, dad? Is he going to be ok?' Daniel asked.

Scott, the youngest, added, 'Can we go see him dad?'

Joe could hardly speak. A lump filled his throat. He bit his lip to stop himself from bursting out crying. He looked across at Helen.

'Of course, Gramps is going to be ok.' She took hold of the conversation. 'Now come on you two … off to bed … and don't forget to say a little prayer.' She rounded the kids up and led them towards the bathroom, 'but brush your teeth first.'

'Can Gramps still take us to the football on Saturday, dad?' Daniel asked again. 'He promised us he would.'

'He did,' added Scott.

'We'll see,' Helen ushered them both into the bathroom.

Joe sat down on the settee and closed his eyes. In his imagination, he pictured the crowd singing at the local football stadium. The two teams running out onto the field. A roar going up. He then visualised his father in a wheelchair, still unconscious, with a football scarf around his neck. Joe trying to pull him up the steps to their seats. His two boys trying to help. The crowd falling silent. The players stopping and staring up at them.

Joe opened his eyes and ripped off his tie. He tossed it across the room.

'Here.' Helen handed him a glass of wine. 'Look Joe … it will be ok. If it comes to the worst, he can stay here.'

He took a large gulp of the wine, almost finishing it in one go. He glared at the carpet in silence.

She hugged him. 'Come on, we can always turn the dining room into his bedroom. We can put a ramp in for the wheelchair.'

'You don't understand,' he muttered.

'It'll be ok … we'll make his life as comfortable as possible.'

In his vivid imagination, the son pictured his father sitting in the corner of the room in a wheelchair with a flashing light Santa's hat on his head. No life in his eyes. His hands dangling down by the side of the chair that held him prisoner.

Joe necked the rest of the alcohol. He slammed the glass down on the table.

'It will be ok, love … I promise.'

‘You don’t understand.’ Heading for the door, Joe grabbed his coat and stormed out of the house.

He wasn’t sure where he was going as he walked through the damp, grey streets. The light rain soaked his face. A woman jogged past him. He passed an old people’s home. He looked through the window. An old man sat perched up in a chair near a television. A nurse stood over him, feeding him. Food dribbled down his chin. He just sat there, staring at the white wall.

With his head spinning like a top, Joe turned and ran through the streets.

Ten minutes later, he sat holding his unconscious father’s hand in the hospital room.

‘Wake up dad … please … wake up … I don’t want you to be like this … it’s not fair … Don’t make me do this …. please, I have a life to live …. a family …. a job… wake up … wake up… I shouldn’t have promised you. Why did I promise you?’

He looked at the life support machine, still bleeping away in the corner. His eyes followed the cord leading to the plug in the wall. There was a sign next to it, stating: - Do not switch off.

He stood up and moved towards it. He looked at his father, then back at the plug. He stood staring, his heart thumped loudly in his chest, his entire body shook.

Suddenly, a nurse walked in. 'Sorry,' she said, 'I didn't know anyone was in here. I'm here to give Mister Lewis his bed bath.'

'It's OK … OK … nurse.' He jumped back from the wall as if he'd had a small electric shock. 'I've got to go anyway.'

Joe kissed his old man on the forehead and left.

Thirty minutes later, Joe sat in one of the wooden pews in the Catholic Church about a mile away from where he lived. He looked around the impressive but unfriendly, cold building. A statue of the Virgin Mary stared down at him.

'Don't judge me,' he muttered under his breath, 'you don't know the half of it.'

An old woman skulked out of the confessional box. With a white handkerchief she wiped a tear from her eyes. She knelt down beside Joe. 'I think it's your turn next,' she whispered, pulling a set of rosary beads from her handbag.

'I guess so.' He took a deep breath and rose to his feet.

Quietly, he entered the small space and knelt down. He could hear the priest breathing heavily through the strip of black cloth positioned in the wooden partition wall.

Joe knelt there in silence. Inside his head, thoughts spun around and around like they were strapped into a carriage on a Waltzer at the fairground.

'When you're ready, my son,' the priest's voice broke the awkward silence.

'Sorry, Father … it's been about.' He tried to do the maths in his head. 'I'm, I'm not really sure how long it's been since my last confession. I'm guessing about twenty-five years or more.'

'Never mind, my son … it's always good to have a stray sheep return to the flock. Carry on.'

Another uncomfortable hush.

'To be honest, Father … it's been so long I can't remember what to say next … can I just get to the point.'

'Of course, you can my son, this is not a test.'

Joe took a deep breath. He still couldn't believe what he was about to say next. He thought about just getting up and walking out.

But he knew he had to talk to someone, he had to tell someone. 'Look Father … I'm going to kill someone.'

The priest coughed cold tea over the floor. 'You are going to do what?'

'Kill someone.'

'Who?'

'My father, Father.'

'Can I ask why?'

Joe thought back to the day in the park with his father and his two kids. It was about five minutes before Daniel and Scott climbed up the steps of the slide. The two boys were running around full of life. Joe and his dad watched an old woman getting wheeled passed them by a younger woman, maybe her daughter, or her carer.

'Hey son,' Ronny spoke, 'if anything happens to me ...'

'Nothing's going to happen to you, dad … you're as fit as a fiddle.'

'I'm not as fit as I was Joe … now listen … I'm just saying if something did …' Joe offered him a mint. 'No thanks … I want you to promise me something.'

'Promise you what?'

'If I ever end up like your mother did … I want you to … to,' he stared into his son's eyes, 'kill me.'

'Shut up.'

'I'm serious.'

'You don't sound it … sounds like you're off your rocker more like.'

'I've never been so serious in my life, son. I saw your mother crippled with dementia. She couldn't remember anything. She couldn't walk; couldn't do anything for herself.'

'I remember dad.'

'Let me finish … she was like a baby …. now when I close my eyes that's my only memory of her … her sitting dribbling … a shell of the person I used to love … and I don't want yours,' he pointed towards the boys, 'or their, memories of me to be like that … so promise me.'

'Promise you what?'

He whispered, 'You will … kill me.'

'Dad … this isn't the Godfather film.'

'Stop making a joke out of this and promise me.'

'No.'

‘Please, Joe … I’ve never asked you for anything in my life before … this is important to me … I’d rather die than be like that … please.’

‘Dad, listen to yourself … you want me to,’ he lowered his voice to a murmur, ‘murder you.’

The father held his son’s hands. He stared at him. ‘It’s not technically murder … but yes, son … it’s important to me.’

‘Ok, it’s your life I guess … Ok I’ll do it.’ Joe told him what he wanted to hear. He didn’t even want to think about his dad getting old, never mind ill. He had no intention of going ahead with it.

‘Do what?’

‘What you just said.’

‘What did I just say?’

‘Dad!’

‘I want to hear you say it.’

‘Ok, ok … if something bad happens to you, and you can’t look after yourself …or blow your nose, or wipe your own arse … I won’t look after you like a normal person would … I will kill you instead … happy now?’

‘Look at us Gramp,’ Daniel shouted down from near the top, waiting for their turn to go.

Ronny waved at them as the brothers slid down together. Ronny turned back to his own son. He held out his hand. Joe looked at it with uncertainty.

‘Ok, son … is it a deal?’

‘Don’t be stupid dad.’

‘Don’t speak to your old man like that … I’m far from stupid … now shake on it.’

Joe reluctantly took his father’s hand in his and they shook.

‘You can never break your promise, son … don’t forget … it’s important to me … ok?’

Joe looked his father in the eyes. They stared at each other for twenty long seconds. ‘OK … dad … I won’t break my promise.’

The two boys appeared from the bottom of the slide. They grabbed their grandfather’s hand. ‘Come on gramps … let’s play football.’

Ronny smiled at his son. ‘Come on then, boys … I’m Georgie Best.’

‘Who’s Georgie Best, Gramps?’ Scott asked.

Joe watched his boys and his father kicking the ball about on the grass. At that moment, he deliberately pushed the promise out of his mind. 'You idiot dad,' he muttered to himself.

Back in the confessional box, the priest pulled back the curtain, but the space was empty. He could hear footsteps hurriedly pacing towards the door. By the time the priest made his way out into the church, he saw the big wooden doors closing. Father John made the sign of the cross, and to the amazement of the old woman, he got down on his knees and started praying.

Joe sneaked back through the hospital ward. He tip-toed past the nurse who sat in the back room, watching tele. Joe opened the door to his father's room and entered. He stood at the edge of the bed, looking down at his father lying there.

Joe held a pillow in his trembling hands. Tears streamed down his face. Slowly he lowered the pillow towards his father's face. He pressed it down hard. There was no struggle at first. Joe looked away while adding more pressure. He felt the life slowly draining out of his father's body. The life support machine stopped bleeping, instead it gave off a constant one decibel hum.

‘I did it, dad … I promised you I would.’ He removed the pillow from his face.

His father’s eyes shot open, his hand gripped Joe’s hand. ‘Thank you, boy … thank you.’

Joe screamed.

All of a sudden, the light in the room switched on. Joe’s two sons and his wife stood in the doorway. A look of shock and horror on their faces.

‘Daddy, why did you kill gramps?’ Daniel spat the words out at his father.

‘Gramper's dead … gramper's dead,’ Scott started crying.

‘Joe … what the hell have you done?’ Helen tried to shield her children from looking. The wine in her wine glass spilled onto the floor.

‘I can explain,’ Joe said.

A nurse walked in. She shrieked and dropped a bedpan. A policeman appeared behind her holding a machine gun from the 1920’s. ‘Drop the pillow, sir.’ He pointed the gun at Joe.

‘You don’t understand, he wanted me to do it … honest … I made him a promise.’

‘Drop the pillow, I said … NOW!’ the copper aimed the weapon at him.

From the corridor, a ringing sound grew louder and louder. Still holding the pillow, Joe walked towards the policeman. ‘But you don’t understand.’

‘Stop, sir.’

‘But I can explain.’

‘Stop Joe … just put the pillow down,’ Helen screamed out.

BANG! BANG! BANG!

The bullets ripped through Joe’s chest.

‘Joe?’ Helen screeched.

‘Daddy,’ the two boys bawled.

Joe clutched his heart and fell on to the bed next to his father. He lay there. The ringing noise grew louder.

‘Arrrggghhhhh,’ Joe’s eyes shot open. He looked about. He lay there in his own bed, in his own bedroom. His wife lay next to him, fast asleep.

‘It was a dream … it was a bloody dream.’ He looked at his wife still sleeping soundly.

From the hallway, the phone rang out. In just his underpants, Joe leapt out of bed and rushed down the stairs.

'Yes,' he replied to the voice on the other end. 'this is Joe Lewis.' He listened as someone spoke. 'Oh … thank you … thank you … I'll be there as soon as I can.'

He placed the phone back down. He looked up at his wife standing at the top of the stairs.

'What's happened, Joe … what's happened?'

'It's my father … he … he … he died in his sleep.'

Helen hugged him. 'I'm so sorry Joe … so sorry.'

Joe began to laugh and laugh. Helen removed her arms from around him. Joe walked into the front room. He took the photo off the wall of his father playing football in the garden with Daniel and Scott.

'Thank you, dad … I love you.'

xxxxxx

SIN

(Before you read this, there is a quick back story that I must explain to you). *Many, many moons ago, God invented Man and named him Adam, after looking into the future and seeing Adam Ant performing Stand and Deliver on Top of the Pops. On witnessing God's new creation, Lucifer was right pissed off and decided to try and copy off him by making his own Man.*

Unfortunately, his demons fucked it up and ended up making a creature that looked slightly similar to Adam but had two big, pillow things on its chest and no warning prick, sorry, stick between its legs. The Prince of Darkness called it Wow-Man and sent it down to the Garden of Eden to destroy the status quo (not the band. I know they are very old but this was even before them lot). At that time there were only male creatures wandering about the earth; playing blow football, having farting competitions, and chilling out by the river. It was perfect. That all changed when Evil Eve started going out with Adam.

It was a boiling hot and sticky day in the Garden of Eden. Relaxing by the meandering river, several of God's creatures lay stretched out on the grass, eating ice-creams and talking about important man stuff.

'I luvs Magnums,' said Clifford the Cheetah.

'Give me a Fab any day,' added Leo the Lion.

Mikey the Monkey took off his sunglasses, 'A 99 for me with a flake and lots of nuts and that red sauce stuff.'

Ollie the Otter leapt up on his short, stubby legs and threw the remains of his choc-ice at a large fish in the water. The otter was angry. He was always angry. 'Never mind all that … what are we going to do about Adam?' he shrieked in an otter kinda squeaky voice. 'He's gone all weird since that … Wow-Man appeared.'

'Jealous, are you?' Leo joked.

The otter bent over, and spread the cheeks of his arse. 'Lick my ring Leo.'

Mikey the Monkey put his sunglasses back on. ‘I don’t agree with most of what the otter says, but on this matter, I think he’s right, Leo. Adam doesn’t bother with us anymore.’

‘I know I’m right,’ spat Ollie, ‘He’s obsessed with Evil Eve. And I don’t trust her.'

‘You don’t trust anyone,’ Leo pointed out.

The cheetah nodded. ‘And he’s always going on about her, “Eve said this and Eve said that.”’

‘He’s the bloody talk of the Jungle. We’ve got to have a word with him!’ Ollie the Otter piped up again.

Just at that moment, Adam walked through a clearing in the forest towards them. In his hand, he held a carrier bag from Aldi (well it looked like it was from Aldi’s but it couldn’t have been, could it?). The human’s hair had been cut short; he wore a tee-shirt with the Devil’s face on it and had a dangly earring in his left ear.

‘A word with who, Ollie?’ Adam smiled.

‘What the fuck?’ said the otter, ‘Where did you get that tee-shirt from?’

‘Eve made it for me … great isn’t it?'

The monkey looked at the label at the back. 'It says' George at Asda', on here.'

'Get off, it doesn't.'

'Oooohhh, look at the fuckin' earring on him as well … he thinks he's David fuckin' Cassidy,' the otter mocked.

Adam twisted his head to show it off. 'Nice ain't it?'

'Nice! You look like a right knob.'

'Shut up, Ollie,' Leo the Lion snapped at him. 'Hey Adam, have you got a minute?' Leo sat next to the man. The big cat placed its massive paw on the man's leg. Its claws cut into his skin. 'Sorry, Adam,'

'Bloody Hell Leo you need your nails cut… and I haven't got time, sorry mate … Eve's cooking tonight. I've got her these spring onions.' He held up the carrier bag.

'Oooooh, I luvs spring onions.' Leo licked his lips.

'Tell him, Leo … tell him.' Ollie nudged him.

'Tell me what?'

Leo stared coldly at the small, furry creature. 'I'll tell him in my own time, Ollie. And stop nudging me or else.'

'Or else what?' the otter shrugged,

The monkey put its hand up. ‘Leo said he would put you in a sack and throw you in the river if you ever nudged him again.’

The otter rolled its eyes. ‘Fuck off, Hairy Mary.’

The cheetah held up a sack with the otter’s name written on it.

‘And you can fuck off too, Spotted Dick.'

‘Well … what is it?’ Adam stood up.

‘It’s about you and this wow-man,’ Leo the Lion nodded his large mane.

‘Eve? What’s wrong with her?’

The otter chipped in. ‘We don’t fuckin’ trust her.’ They all glared at the otter. ‘Well … we don’t … she doesn’t even have a warning prick, sorry, stick … it’s not natural.’ He clutched his groin to prove a point.

Adam laughed loudly and slapped his leg ‘So? The slug doesn’t have a warning stick either but you trust him.’

‘He’s right,’ said Mikey the Monkey.

‘Yeah, but I didn’t see the slug with a 14-inch cucumber hanging halfway out of his glove compartment last week.’

‘You didn’t see Eve do that,’ Adam piped up.

The otter looked him squarely in the eye. ‘I did … right up to the tip.’

‘Shut up, Ollie.’

‘But Adam mun, we never see you anymore,’ Mikey the Monkey said. ‘We used to have so much fun. Remember the butt burping contests?' The Monkey tried to force wind from its pink puckered behind.

‘Good times, Mike … but life moves on.’

‘And she walks funny. She walks exactly like him,’ the otter pointed at Clifford the Cheetah.

‘I don’t walk funny. Do I?’ The cheetah looked at the lion. ‘Do I Leo? Do I Mikey?’

The lion ignored him. ‘Adam, we are just making sure that you aren't making a big mistake with this wow-man. She did appear out of thin air.’

‘Just cos Eve saunters around like the cheetah, doesn’t mean she’s evil,’ Adam snapped back.

Clifford’s jaw dropped open. ‘I knew it! Why didn’t someone tell me I walked funny? You're supposed to be my friends.’ He tried to walk in a straight line, while looking at his behind at the same time.

‘Clifford … shut up,’ Leo the Lion cried, ‘this is important.’

‘What Leo and having a funny walk isn’t important? Anything else about me now, boys?'

‘Yeah,’ the otter retorted, ‘you’re a wanker.’ He turned back to the human. ‘What about the snake, Adam? I definitely don’t trust the snake.’ The otter folded his little arm things.

Adam was losing his temper. He was starting to despise the otter with its endless questioning. ‘What has the snake got to do with it?’

The lion spoke. ‘Eve spends a lot of time talking quietly with the reptile Adam … lots of time.’

‘You’re all jealous of her … that’s all.’

‘Look, Adam,’ the lion’s voice was calm and soothing, ‘we're just making sure that you aren't making a big mistake. We don’t want you to mess things up with God.’

Adam tried to laugh again. This time it didn’t have the same ring of confidence to it. ‘Look, there’s nothing wrong with Eve. She’s not evil … she wouldn't hurt a firefly.' Adam stormed off back toward his home.

'Leo … Leo,' the monkey tried to catch the lion's attention

'What is it, Mikey?'

'Adam forgot his spring onions … should I chase after him?' The monkey held up the bag full of vegetables.

'No, no, no … leave them.' The lion licked its lips. 'I'll see he gets them.'

About three miles away, in Adam and Eve's small-holding at the edge of the forest, Eve stood by a homemade table stirring some kind of homemade soup. On a branch nearby Stan the slimy Snake watched her every move.

'What do you think?' She gave him a little taste.

Through gritted teeth, Stan the Snake replied, 'Hummmmm … nicesssssssss.' When she looked away, he spat the soup out. 'How are you and Adam getting along?' he changed the subject.

'Don't tell Lucifer but I think he's quite yummy … lovely rear end on him.' Her cheeks blushed.

‘That’s good to hear. So, isn’t it time you took it to the next level with him?

‘Do you mean?’ She leant in to him and whispered in his ear.

The snake moved away from her sharply and gave her a stare as if she had farted in a bag and put it over his head. ‘No … I didn’t mean that … good God, are you sick or something … arrghhhhh … why would you do that?’

‘I read it in here.’ She held up a copy of Cosmo.

‘No, give him a surprise I meant.’

‘But that would surprise him,’ she winked at him.

‘That would surprise the fuckin’ singer from Soft Cell … Oh I can’t stop thinking of it now! I meant maybe cook him a special meal … with something nice for him to drink.’

‘Oh, I see …. what type of meal?’

‘Come in closer and let me show you.’ He held up a copy of Jamie Oliver’s Cookbook for Dummies or The Working Class.

She listened. A cute smile curled up her lips. ‘That sounds neat.’

Stan the Snake crawled off. A long snakey sneer on his long snakey face. He knew Lucifer would be pleased.

Eve took the large knife and sauntered around the back of the house whistling a New Order song.

Adam had barely simmered down by the time he arrived back at their small-holding. In the sky the orange-tinged sun had just about set, while in the opposite corner the moon sat, waiting impatiently for its chance to come out and show its cheesy grin.

'Eve,' Adam yelled out. His catcall was met with silence. He tried again. 'EVE … EVE?' Adam could smell something unusual, but rather enticing floating on the warm air. 'The onions! Oh shit!' he cursed the animals for sidetracking him. 'Oh well,' he thought, 'small mercies.' He knew the strongly flavoured root vegetables played havoc with Eve's digestive system. Last time she ate them she sounded like a tugboat lost in fog, and smelled like a wild warthog after it had eaten an out of date, Chicken Tikka Masala from the Co-Op.

'Hi Adam,' came a reply from behind the palm tree door that fronted Eve's hut. 'I'll be there now in a minute. Take a seat.'

He looked across at the dinner table which was set and adorned with flowers. Two wooden plates and two glasses fashioned out of tropical leaves sat on top. A firefly balancing on the edge of one of the yellow flowers got ready to start an evening of flying about in the dark and blinking like an indicator of a car about to turn left.

'What's all this Eve?' Adam shouted out.

'A special surprise,' she yelled back. 'I just wanted to do something nice for you.' She didn't mention who had suggested it.

He winked at the firefly. The fly winked back and set off on its evening journey. Adam looked on in awe as the little insect lit up, and glided smoothly through the night air.

CRASH!

It flew straight into the path of the door as Eve opened it. The dazed insect fell to the earth, its light dimly twinkling.

Unaware of the damage she had caused, the wow-man sashayed out from her hut. She handed him a package wrapped tightly in brown, autumn leaves. He eagerly ripped it open like a kid on Christmas morning. He held it up, a baffled expression on his face. 'It's lo…lo…lovely!' he commented. 'What is it?'

‘It’s something to cover you up down there.’ She nodded towards his lower region. ‘I call it a thong.’

If truth be told, she had made it because she was sick of seeing his warning prick, sorry, stick coming to life every time she strolled past. ‘It’s to stop you from rubbing your floppy bit on stingy nettles,’ she fibbed.

She helped him put on the thong which consisted of two long pieces of reed, found by the river and fixed to either side of a fig leaf. She placed it between his legs and tied it around his hips. He walked gingerly over to the hut and back. He felt stupid and he knew the other guys would take the mickey out of him. Especially Ollie the Otter, the little, hairy shit.

‘Well what do you think?’ she said. He could see the delight in her eyes

‘It rides up a bit.’ He struggled to pull an itchy bit of fig leaf from out of the crack of his arse. A painful expression spread across his face.

False tears filled up in her eyes. ‘You don’t like it, do you?’

‘No, Eve … sorry, yes, I do! It’s great… but I’m not sure what God will think. He doesn’t like things like this.’

‘He will. He will probably want one himself,’ she beamed and added, ‘Ok, let me help you take it off. I’ll add a few more reeds in the morning to make it a little bigger.’

She untied the sides and it slid from between his legs. He felt her warmth against his skin. His heart missed a beat. Their faces drew close together. He could smell her breath. It gave off a dry, but sensual aroma. He breathed in her essence. She stared into his eyes. He reached down and instinctively stroked the soft, lumpy things on her chest. He liked them. He wished he had a pair to jiggle around when he was bored. She purred; like a pussy cat after licking the last drop of cream from the bowl. Their faces moved closer, lips automatically reaching out for one another. His warning prick, sorry, stick pointed upwards and touched her belly button. She moaned, he groaned.

Out of the tree, the snake fell from a high branch, landing by their feet. Startled, they jumped apart. The moment ruined.

‘Sorry,’ the snake apologized. ‘I must have dozed off and lost my grip.’ It lied. In truth, it just didn’t want them getting too friendly, too soon. It had a job to do, and the sooner it was done, the sooner he would get six, long legs and a nice pair of ears like Lucifer had promised him. 'Sorry, again.' It slithered away, apologizing repeatedly. The firefly still lay dazed on the ground. It looked at the snake, its eyes pleading for help. The reptile shot its tongue out and swallowed the firefly before sliding back into the shadows.

Eve felt strange, all flustered. Her cheeks glowing red. 'Oh … oh … yes … I've got another surprise for you. Sit down … sit down.'

He sat on the wooden chair trying to hide the embarrassment that throbbed between his legs.

She topped up his glass with a bright red substance.

He gulped it down. 'That's tasty … what is it?' His heart was still pounding in his chest, like a bass drum being banged by an elephant with a club-foot.

She ignored his question. 'If you thought that was good … wait until you taste the grub I made.'

'Don't tell me you made me asparagus stew … my favourite.' He tied a palm leaf around his neck.

'You'll see. Now close your eyes.'

He did what he was told. She lifted up his chin. 'Open up.' He lowered his bottom jaw. A warm succulent substance was placed on his tongue. She put her hand to his jaws to stop him from spitting it out.

It had an unusual texture. He began to chew. Juices ran down his throat, and trickled down his chin. He started to chomp on it savagely; his taste buds exploded into life.

'More … more,' he demanded. He opened his eyes to see a slab of reddish-pink stuff on the homemade plate. He shovelled the food into his mouth. Saliva dribbled down his chin. She handed him the cup containing the bright red liquid. He swallowed more. He sat silently as he ate and drank, enthralled with the new sensations.

After he'd finished, he lay back in his chair, hands on the back of his head. 'That was the best meal I have ever eaten. It tasted better than bread from Heaven … and the drink, wow! That was wonderful … what were they?'

She fiddled with a new pair of cooking gloves she had ordered from Grattan Catalogue. Only £1.34 a week for 157 weeks. 'Well … I wanted to do something new for you … so I cooked that little, round pink thing.'

Adam tried to recall all the fruits and vegetables of that colour in the Garden of Eden. 'Little, round, pink fruit?' He searched his mind, wishing he had a copy of the Good and Safe Food Guide, Angel Gabriel had promised him, to hand.

She placed another slab of the pink stuff on his plate. He took another bite. 'What pink thing? I can't remember seeing any pink things in the garden like that,' he inquired.

'You know,' she replied, 'that dirty, lazy thing that rolls about in the mud all day and messes up my floor.'

'What … Percy the Pig?' he joked. It wasn't meant to be taken seriously. She didn't smile, her eyes quickly moved downward to study the ground.

His blood ran cold from his head to his toes. His mouth dropped open. He didn't really want to ask the next question, but he had to. 'Eve … tell me you didn't kill … and then actually cook Percy the Pig, did you?'

She stood quietly, staring down. He asked her again. 'Did you?'

She could tell by the tone of his voice that she had made a big mistake. She tried to justify her actions. 'Well you "actually" ate it,' she made a point of emphasising the word "actually". 'And "you" said it was the best meal you had ever tasted.' She placed her hands on her bare-naked hips.

'Eve … I didn't realize the meal consisted of one of my best friends! I thought it was a hard-coated tulip or something.' He jumped to his feet, trying to make himself sick.

Panic set in. The Lord's words knocked loudly at the door of his consciousness: 'There will be no meat-eaters on Earth, Adam … everyone will only eat fruit … only eat fruit, including you Adam! UNDERSTAND?'

Eve tried her best to remedy the situation. 'Don't worry … it was only a pig … have some more pomegranate juice.'

Adam's world came to a grinding halt. He gripped the edge of the table with both hands to steady himself. 'What juice did you say?' The corners of his lips quivered.

'Pomegranate juice … you know, that special fruit off the Tree Full of Knowledge and Goosegoggs, or whatever it is called.' She stood in front of him, holding the container full of the bright red liquid.

'Do you mean The Tree of Knowledge of Good and Evil?' he said slowly. She nodded. 'The tree that I told you never, ever, ever to touch?' She nodded again. His hands curled into fists at his sides. Adrenaline pumped through his veins.

She giggled nervously. 'Yeah. What's that all about? The Tree of Knowledge of Good and Evil - sounds like another crappy Dan Brown novel.'

His heart beat faster and faster. 'You're winding me up.' He replaced his frown with a wide grin. 'You and the pig are having a laugh … you pair of Jokers!' He did his best to convince himself that it was all a bad prank. 'You've Punked me … or Pigged me.' He laughed out loud.

'I haven't, honest,' she replied. 'Here's his head.' She held it up. A light bulb stuck out of the dead animal's mouth. 'I made it into a bedside lamp.'

'Do you know what this means?'

'Yeah … now we can both read in bed.'

'No, you evil bitch … he's going to kick us out. '

'Who?'

'Well, it's not Hector the fuckin' Hippo, is it! God, God will, the one who made us … remember?'

She didn't want to aggravate the situation even more by telling him that she had been made by the Devil. 'Maybe he doesn't need to know.'

'Who?'

'Well, it's not Hector the fuckin' Hippo is it! God, isn't it? … You are so thick sometimes!'

Adam ran towards her. His arms outstretched. He started to strangle her over the table. 'Have you gone mad? Do you know what this means?' Questions shot out of his mouth. She whacked him on the side of his face with Percy's head. He fell back, bumping up against a tree. He started to pace back and forth manically.

'Yeah,' I do know,' she replied, 'I won't have to clean dirty trotter prints off my grass carpet anymore.' A smug look sat on her face.

'No! You evil wow-man … he's going to kick us out.'

'Who is?'

'Not this again … God … God is … you dull bitch! '

'But the snake said he wouldn't mind. It said that God bloke was too busy to worry about Earth, and some fruit, and a smelly pig.'

Adam screamed at the top of his lungs.

Somewhere in the garden, Mikey the Monkey turned to Leo the Lion and said, 'I told you she wouldn't be happy about him forgetting the spring onions.'

Adam dropped to his knees and started to pray. 'Please God … please … please.' His mouth felt dry, his tongue stuck to his teeth. He didn't know what else to say.

Eve interrupted. 'But hang on, he doesn't need to know.

He leaped to his feet and ran towards her, but tripped over a log and fell face down into the dirt.

She added. 'The fruit will grow back before God comes down here to see us.'

He slowly got to his feet; one side of his face plastered with dirt. He placed his hand on his chin and rubbed it. 'OK. That may work … but what about the pig? Pigs don't grow on trees you know.'

A puzzled expression shot across her features. 'Well, the snake told me they do.'

'And you call me thick?'

A wooden plate spun through the air, hit Adam on the head. 'Don't mock me,' she shrieked.

As he lay flat on the ground, thoughts raced through his mind. 'We need to get rid of the evidence.'

'That's no problem, you've already eaten it. All that's left is his head which is now a lovely bedside lamp.'

'OK … OK … we'll hide the head and lamp combo and then pretend you didn't kill, and cook one of God's creatures.'

'You ate it though.'

'You killed it though.'

'You ate it though.'

'But you killed it though.'

'But you ate it though.'

'Eve … Have you always got to have the last word?'

There was a brief silence.

'No … though.'

He picked up a sack and a large knife. He started to stride back out into the dense forest.

'What are you going to do?' she asked.

'Going to have a long chat with that sleazy snake.' Adam paced off into the undergrowth. He yelled back. 'And when I'm gone try not to kill and cook anything else … right?'

'I bet you'll eat it though,' she shouted back.

*****

CHANCE

'No… no … no, not another musical,' Dan paced around the student's common room, shaking his head. 'I couldn't stick another oneeeeeee… please lord.'

'Why not?' Hannah knew how to wind up her classmate.

So did her best friend, Sarah, who had already started to sing-a-long to Hakuna Matata. Her voice sailing high above the din of the radio playing in the corner.

Matilda who was standing by the counter, waiting for the kettle to boil, joined in, quickly followed by Hannah. They all aimed their voices towards Dan.

'That's why bloody not,' he buried his head in his hands. They all laughed. 'Look,' he added, 'how about a drama … something gritty, maybe with knives or …… guns … or …'

‘Here we go … Dan the gangster.’

‘Shut up, Hannah.’

‘Yeah … Dan the gangster maaaaaaaaaan.’

‘And you can too, Sarah.’

Dan slumped down in his chair. The girls all burst out laughing again.

In a nearby park, a fifteen-year-old boy and his girlfriend sat on the swings looking at a funny video on the boy’s mobile phone.

‘Play it again,’ the girl laughed.

From out of the trees, Lewis Morgan sauntered towards them, cigarette in his mouth. Dark glasses covering his darker eyes. He grabbed the phone out of the boy’s hand.

‘Oh.’ The lad got to his feet.

Lewis pushed him backwards and glared at him.

‘Hey, that’s his phone … give it back you dickhead,’ the girl shouted.

Lewis pushed his face into hers. A snarl turned up his top lip. ‘Well, it’s mine now.’ He blew her a kiss.

‘Leave her alone, and give me my phone back.’

‘What?’

'You heard.'

Lewis grabbed the boy by the throat and squeezed. He removed his sunglasses, his eyes bulging wildly. He tightened his grip. 'You want some?'

The boy struggled to answer. He shook his head. Lewis released his stranglehold. Clutching his throat, the boy collapsed on one knee.

'Thought so.' Lewis added, before walking off through the gates of the park.

Without looking, he stepped out into the main road. A car skidded, missing the youth by a few inches. Lewis stopped, turned and flicked his fag nip at the car windscreen. The driver beeped the horn and shook his fist. Lewis laughed loudly and sauntered off towards the college.

Back in the common room, the four media students were still sitting around, discussing and making suggestions for their next production.

'Let's do a comedy then.' Dan clapped his hands.

'You must be joking' Sarah shook her head. 'Us … lot … there's more comedy in a brick.'

Dan looked at the glum faces of the girls, and slightly disheartened he muttered, ‘Maybe you’re right this time, Laurel - or is it Hardy?'

It was Sarah’s turn to punch him lightly in the arm. Matilda poured the boiling water into the mugs. The teabags floated to the top. She wandered over towards the three of them sitting in a circle, leaving the tea on the counter to brew.

‘I’ve got an idea,’ she chipped in.

They turned to look at her. She sat down with them. In the doorway, Lewis lurked.

‘What about a ghost story?’ Matilda added.

‘A ghost story?’ Hannah replied.

‘Oooooooooo,’ Dan tickled her.

‘Get off.’

Matilda elaborated, ‘Did you know this place is haunted?’

‘What is? The college? No way.’ Dan scoffed.

‘Yeah, honest … apparently, there’s two ghosts who live here. A good ghost who protects us actors …’

Lewis entered the room and walked towards the counter. Matilda continued, 'And then there's a bad one … She feeds on evil people … very evil people.'

They looked at Lewis.

'Lewis,' Dan piped up, 'I thought you would be in prison by now.'

'Sit on this.' Lewis's middle finger saluting Dan caused the girls to shake their heads in disgust.

'That's not nice Lewis Morgan,' Hannah said.

Thinking he would impress them; Lewis pulled a big bag of pills out of his jacket. 'Talking about ghosts, girls … one of these and you'll see all the ghouls you want.'

Matilda folded her arms. 'Go away Lewis … we're trying to write a new play.'

'Can I help?' He appeared quite genuine.

'No.'

'Come on, I've got some really nasty ideas for a ghost story,' Lewis tried to put on his best creepy voice.

'No, Lewis, we don't want to hear your ideas.' Hannah turned her back on him. The others did the same and carried on having their own conversation.

Biting his lip, the thug marched over to the fridge.

'Who's he?' Sarah, the new student, asked. 'I haven't seen him around here before.'

Hannah whispered. 'Him … he's in the year above us … good actor to be honest … but he's trouble.'

'Yeah,' Dan added, 'with a huge Capital T.'

Lewis opened the fridge, pulled out the milk and gulped down the liquid straight from the plastic bottle. He reached across and turned the radio up

The other teenagers sat in the circle chatting. Matilda continued with her story, 'Apparently, rumour has it that when the bad ghost was alive … she was badly bullied by others.'

'How long ago was that?' asked Sarah.

'In the 1950's … when this place first opened.'

'I didn't realise the college was open that long ago.'

'No … it wasn't a college then … it used to be a TB hospital for kids who suffered from the disease.'

'I didn't know that … those poor, poor children.' Sarah piped up.

Hannah agreed.

'Can we continue with the ghost story please?'

'Ok, Dan … anyway, rumour has it that this small gang of older kids in the hospital dragged this poor girl down into the old cellar.'

'Why?'

'They claimed she was some kind of evil witch.'

'Bollocks,' Lewis, who was listening by the counter, muttered a little too loudly. They all turned to look at him. 'Well, it is.' He shrugged.

'We are not talking to you Lewis,' Hannah spoke up.

They all turned back to face Matilda. As she told the story, the others could almost picture the scene taking place years before. A gang of kids in weird clothes and some wearing masks, pushing the girl down the cold, concrete steps into a dark, damp cellar, near where the theatre now stood.

'Is that, that small door which is always locked?' Hannah asked.

'Yes.'

'I always get goose pimples when I walk past that,' Hannah disclosed.

'Me too,' Sarah revealed, and shivered on saying it.

Matilda resumed. 'The poor girl wrestled to break free. 'Get off … get off me,' she screamed.

The other kids ignored her pleas. They seemed to be in some kind of trance. They kept chanting, 'Katie is a witch … Katie is a witch.'

'They pulled and pushed her down into the pitch-black cellar. There she cowered, sobbing in the corner like a wounded dog.'

'The gang hissed at her like snakes, and left her curled up in a ball in the darkness. They locked the cellar door and didn't tell anyone where she was. The people in charge assumed she had run away.'

'What happened to her?' Hannah asked. Her and Sarah sat there holding hands with each other. Even Dan appeared lost for words.

Matilda lowered her voice to almost a whisper. 'She hung herself down there. No one found her for over three months. Now, the story goes, she hides there, rope still around her neck … waiting … waiting … for revenge.

They all looked out towards the corridor where the cellar door stood bolted.

Sarah was the first to speak. 'OMG, ... that's terrible.'

At the back of the room, Lewis sighed. 'Good ghosts, bad ghosts … what a bunch of cry-babies.' He looked around to make sure they weren't looking at him, before carefully dropping a tablet into each of the mugs of tea. Feeling quite pleased with himself, he ambled out, whistling.

'That is a great story, mind.' Dan walked over to the counter. He removed the tea bags and carried the tray of teas back to the group.

Grinning like a Cheshire cat, Lewis walked along the corridor, past the entrance to the small 100-seater purpose-built theatre which had been commissioned with funding from the Lottery, when they converted the derelict building into a Media and Arts college ten years earlier. He stopped and stared at the cellar door.

'Ooohhhhhh, anyone down there?' He booted the old wooden slats. Silence. 'Thought not … I need a piss.'

He entered the toilet cubicle and closed the door. Even though smoking was banned, he lit up a cigarette and started fiddling with the stolen phone.

Down in the cellar, an eerie grey light pulsed away in the corner. The light got brighter and brighter. It twirled and spun, and then scuttled across the dark cellar room, up the stairs and smashed into the cellar door.

BANG!

The cellar door buckled. A set of drawers in a cupboard out in the corridor opened and closed by themselves. The noise caused Lewis to drop his fag onto the toilet floor.

'Hello?' he spoke, his eyes checking the confined space, 'Who's that?'

The noise grew louder and louder. The cellar door rattled and shook. Lewis cupped his hands around his ears to block out the terrible sound. He found himself backing up against the toilet wall.

Then suddenly, everything went silent.

Pulling his trousers up, Lewis sprinted out of the cubicle into the corridor. He looked at the cellar door and froze on seeing someone's eye looking out of a hole in the wooden slats. Lewis felt too scared to cry out. He turned and fled down the corridor. He stopped in his tracks and looked down at his clothes.

'What the fuck?' They weren't the clothes he had on earlier. They were old and torn. Like clothes kids wore in Dickens's day.

A thud like a loud heartbeat bled through the entire building. A clock on the wall by the entrance fell crashing to the floor. The cellar door started banging again. The bolt struggling to keep whatever it was behind the door from bursting out. A boy on all fours wearing a dog mask came crawling out of one of the classrooms. He barked at Lewis and bounded towards him.

Lewis ran into the common room. He slipped on the floor. Scrambling to his feet, he slammed the common room door shut behind him. He peeked through the glass. 'What's fuckin' going on guys?' he said.

Silence.

He turned around slowly. Chairs lay strewn across the floor; all the mugs were smashed. The table lay on its side. The four college students he had only left a few minutes ago were nowhere to be seen. Instead, a girl with bandages over her eyes, dressed like a Victorian Doll sat playing the piano in the corner. A scary looking man with a bald head, dressed in a monk's cowl sat on a weird wooden statue in the centre of the room.

Lewis gulped. 'Oh, who are you? Where's the others gone?'

The man just stared at him. Lewis was petrified, too frightened to move. The man pointed at the boy and spoke, 'Last chance … last chance.'

The girl playing the piano banged the keys hard with her fists, blood seeped through the bandages covering her eyes. She opened her mouth to smile at Lewis. A spider crawled out of it and landed on top of the piano keys.

Lewis screamed. He clambered to open the door and fell back out onto the floor in the corridor. The entrance to the building was bricked up. Loud moans and groans escaped from inside the theatre. He headed towards there, looking over his shoulder.

He almost fell through the curtains into the theatre space. It was pitch-black. A gang of weird-looking teenagers sat in the seats. One held up an umbrella. Several wore masks; one girl had blood over her face. They all sat still, staring straight ahead. A spotlight lit up the stage. The scary man from the common room stood staring out at the rows of seats.

'Lewis … we've been waiting for you. Take a seat.'

Lewis ignored him and turned and headed back to the exit. From nowhere, the scary man stood next to him. 'Sit down … I said … NOW!'

The boy did what he was told. He squeezed into a seat in the fifth row. The man disappeared. The boy wearing the dog mask, crawled across the floor and growled at Lewis. Lewis drew his legs up onto the chair.

A series of bright lights brought the stage to life. Lewis rubbed his eyes on seeing the three teenage girls sitting around the table in the common room, talking about the play they were going to write. Dan walked back from the counter, carrying the tray of teas. He handed them out to the girls.

Hannah placed her mug on the table. 'Ok, let's do the ghost story. Who will be the main characters?' She produced a pen and some paper, and started to jot ideas down on a pad. Sarah took a large sip of her tea.

'Hannah, you can play the bad ghost,' Dan joked.

'Why me?'

'Cos you are so baaaaaaaaaad,' he laughed. She punched him in his arm. 'See?' he added. 'You're evil.'

'Shut up Dan.'

Sarah took another sip before placing her mug on the table. 'I don't feel well … I feel …' she tried to stand up, but fell to the floor. Her entire body was shaking.

Hannah screamed.

'What's wrong with her? What's wrong with her?' Matilda cried out.

BOOSH!

On the stage, the lights blacked out.

CLICK.

A single spotlight, shone on Lewis sitting in the audience. All the weird teenagers turned in their seats to stare at him.

BOOSH!

The stage again lit up. This time, two ambulance men rushed on from the wings. They both tried to save the girl convulsing on the floor. Her friends stood holding hands in silence.

BOOSH!

Lights went off for the second time. Lewis sat there, biting his nails. All eyes were fixed on him. He thought about making a run for it. He looked at the exit but the scary man stood guarding it. He shook his bald head at the boy. His eyes were almost blood red.

BOOSH!

On the brightly lit stage, the three students stood silently, looking down at the blanket covering the dead girl on the floor.

BOOSH

Lights black out again. Dog boy bit out at Lewis's ankle. Someone behind the thug tried to grab his head. Lewis screamed.

BOOSH!

On the stage, Sarah's mother walked on. A photo of her daughter clutched in her hand. One of Sarah's older sisters appeared by her side and put her arm around her mother's shoulders.

'Who would have done this?' the mother cried out, 'Who would have killed my little girl?'

From the edge of the stage, Hannah looked out into the audience and picked out Lewis. Hatred spread across her features. 'It was him … him.'

Matilda joined in. 'He did it … Lewis did it.'

'Lewis did it.' Dan points as well. 'He drugged her … he drugged her.'

The dog boy snapped at Lewis's leg again.

'Fuck off,' he kicked out.

Everyone on the stage walked to the edge and chanted at Lewis, 'He did it … he did it.'

Lewis shook his head, 'I didn't mean it. I only wanted to …'

The rest of the teenagers crawled over the seats towards him. They groaned, they moaned like zombies; they spat their displeasure out at him.

Lewis cowered deep down in the chair, hands over his face. He started sobbing like a baby. 'Forgive me … forgive me … I just wanted to be friends with them … They wouldn't let me get involved … I won't ever do it again … honest.'

The old, scary man appeared in the seat next to him. He grabbed the boy's face. 'See what you would have done … see.' His eyes burned into Lewis's brain.

'I'm sorry … sorry,' the youth muttered.

'This is a warning, your last chance,' the man grunted. 'Lucky for you it was me … not Katie.'

Outside the theatre, the door to the cellar rattled.

BOOSH.

Silence.

All the lights in the theatre came on. Lewis shielded his eyes from the glare. When his eyes readjusted, he found himself sitting alone in the empty theatre. He sat there wearing his original clothes.

Slightly dazed and confused, the youth got up and strolled out through the theatre door. As if by magic, he found himself back in the common room. The four students sat in a circle discussing the play they were going to write. Lewis walked over to Sarah, and gently poked her in the arm. 'You're alive!'

'What?'

'Nothing … can I help you guys … I've got some good ideas.'

Hannah piped up. 'No Lewis … we don't want to hear your ideas.'

'Please … I,' he looked about, 'I need to….'

'We said no … we don't want your kind in our play…so beat it.'

Matilda folded her arms. 'Go away Lewis … we're trying to write.'

Lewis bit his lip. He marched over to the fridge.

'Who's he?' Sarah, the new student, asked. 'I haven't seen him around here before.'

Hannah whispered. 'Him … he's in the year above us … good actor to be honest … but he's trouble.'

'Yeah,' Dan added, 'with a huge Capital T.'

Lewis opened the fridge, pulled out the milk and gulped down the liquid straight from the plastic bottle. He reached across and turned the radio up. The other teenagers sat in the circle chatting.

Matilda continued, 'Apparently, rumour has it that when the bad ghost was alive … she was badly bullied by others.' Matilda lowered her voice to almost a whisper to end her story. 'She hung herself down there. No one found her for over three months. Now the story goes, she hides there, rope still around her neck … waiting … waiting … for revenge.'

They all looked out towards the corridor, where the cellar door stood bolted.

'I can help … honest.' Lewis said, 'I've seen the good ghost.'

'High on your drugs are you Lewis, boy,' Dan mocked.

'He's such a knob,' Hannah chipped in.

They laughed and continued in their little huddle.

Lewis whispered to himself. 'Nothing changes … tossers!'

He opened the bag of pills, pulled a few out and started dropping them into the mugs. The dark, scary man appeared by his side and grabbed his hand.

'That was your last chance … I did warn you … boy!'

By his hair, he dragged Lewis to the door and pushed him out into the corridor. The man slammed the door shut on him. The four teenagers in the room carried on talking as if nothing unusual was happening around them.

Lewis banged on the door. 'Let me in … let me in … Dan … Hannah … please.'

The scary man stared at him through the glass. He brought his hand up and waved at the boy.

At that second, the cellar doors started shaking. The drawers of the cupboards in the corridor again started opening and closing by themselves. Lewis turned and looked over his shoulder. The noise became louder.

The bolt holding the cellar door closed, disengaged from the wooden slats. The door shot open, something raced up from the cellar out into the corridor.

Lewis screamed out and tried to run the other way. He slipped on the floor, kicking out at the hand inching towards him.

'Get away … get away.'

The girl's hand grabbed the youth's ankle and wrapped the end of the rope around it. There was a brief silence as Lewis looked at the face of Katie. He could see the other end of the rope attached around her neck. Her face white, bones showing through her skin. She leered at him.

He just stared at her, afraid to move.

WHOOSH.

The girl turned and raced towards the cellar door, dragging the boy with her. He screamed, he yelled; he dug his fingers into the floor to halt his progress. His fingernails were ripped off; a trail of blood led across the corridor floor to the cellar.

Ghost and boy bounced down the concrete stairs. The cellar door slammed closed. The bolt somehow reattached to the wooden slat.

Silence.

Back in the common room, the teenagers sat around the table. Unawares to them, the good ghost sat in the corner watching them.

Hannah said to the others, 'Tell you what, gang … let's actually hear what Lewis's ideas are? Lewis. Lewis?'

They all looked round. Lewis was nowhere to be seen.

'Trust him, he's left the bloody fridge door open,' Dan shook his head.

Unseen by them, the old scary man kicked the tray over, spilling all the drugged teas onto the floor.

'Look what you did now Dan.' Hannah snapped at him.

'I didn't touch it,' he replied.

'You must have … now go and make us a fresh cup … and get the mop.'

The good ghost grinned to himself and ambled out into the corridor to continue his hourly walk around.

******

BOTTLE

'Marry me.'

'What?'

'You heard me.' Down on one knee, underneath the railway arches in downtown Chicago, Jerome held his hands out as if praying.

His girlfriend, Keisha, stood on a large concrete plinth that housed one of the rusty iron stanchions, looking down at him.

The sun beat down on an unusually balmy and hot day for early May. The sidewalks gave the impression they were about to melt into pools of blackest asphalt. Overhead, the train chugging away sounded like it was on its last legs.

'Well … I'll need a ring,' she joked, wiggling her finger near his face.

Looking around, he reached in a rubbish bin and pulled out a Pepsi can. He fiddled with the top until the ring-pull came away. 'Here.' He placed it gently on her finger 'Now will you, Keisha Bonner, take me, Jerome Jackson, to be your husband.' He went down on one knee for the second time.

Across the street, a gang of six, black kids sauntered past. The leader, in a white wife beater vest and baggy jeans, motioned towards the couple. 'Hey JJ, that's where you belong man … down in the dirt.' He spat on the ground. 'I remember when you were a proper man … not a lovesick pussy.' He laughed. The rest of his gang followed suit.

Keisha squeezed her boyfriend's hand. 'Don't take any notice,' she whispered. She could almost feel the tension flowing through his veins.

The two boys stared at each other for several seconds. It was obvious there had been history between them.

Devon smirked before turning away. 'Let's go, boys.' Him and his posse tramped off towards the centre of town.

Jerome watched the gang he'd once hung out with disappear out of sight. They had all grown up together, in the same neighbourhood. He used to be best mates with Devon, childhood blood brothers in fact, but that had all changed when Devon got deeper and deeper into crime. Stealing, muggings, stabbings and beatings became part of his everyday life. Jerome didn't want any part of it, and he had walked away from their friendship rather than getting involved. From what he had seen and heard, Devon was now a ticking time bomb, totally out of control.

'So, will you marry me?' he asked his girlfriend again, a wide grin on his face.

Keisha turned to him. 'But we're only seventeen, Jerome. We have all of our long lives to get married.'

'But I love you babe … with all my heart. I want us to live together forever … until the day I die … have babies together … hundreds of babies.' He seemed so genuine.

'Hundreds?'

'OK … three … maybe four yeah?'

She felt touched. She stared at the sharp piece of metal showcasing her slender finger. 'Ok, Jerome, but you will have to get me a fancier ring than that … a real fine piece of rock … diamonds and rubies … I want the biggest engagement ring in the store.'

He slipped his hands in his pockets. They were empty except for two dollars and a pack of gum. He knew that without a job it would be a long while before he saved enough money to give her what she wanted. But he was determined.

'One day … one day … soon,' he replied.

Hand in hand, they strolled back towards Fourth and Eleventh Street to grab a soda. The warm rays of the sun clung to their backs. Smiles locked on to their happy faces.

A few blocks over, Devon paced in front of the others. Attitude and aggression burst out of every pore in his short, but stocky seventeen-year-old frame. The youth looked every bit the part of a thug, with a shaven head and a scar on his lower lip. Being dragged up on the rough side of the tracks shouldn't have been an excuse for his behaviour, but maybe it went some way toward explaining his attitude problem. One of six kids to a black father, who was now in prison, and a heroin junkie white mother, who spent most of her life lost in her own drug induced world, he had learnt to look after himself and grow up fast and hard, in the tough old streets surrounding Chicago. He wasn't scared of anyone. He'd fight anybody who got in his way; black, white, Mexican, Chinese, it didn't matter to him; they were all his enemies.

'What we gonna to do, man?' one of his cronies asked.

'Let's do the chink's shop … it's like taking candy from a baby,' someone else piped up. With one eye on their leader the rest of the gang nodded.

Devon didn't react, he paced on in front, deep in thought. The gang turned around the corner and into the street. There they came face to face with two police officers. The much older and fatter of the two cops stopped the gang.

'Where are you going, boys?' A thick Irish accent accompanied the words out of his mouth. He fixed his stare on Devon.

'Just around Officer McCormack,' one of the boys replied.

Packed full of hate, Devon glared at the young rookie cop by his partner's side. The rookie looked down at the ground. Devon could almost taste and smell the fear in him. 'That's some real pussy-whipped, candy-ass chicken-shit,' the boy thought to himself.

The older Irish officer poked Devon in his powerful chest. 'Make sure you lot stay outta trouble … understand?'

The boy didn't even bother to answer. He just stared at them both as the officers walked past.

'Ok, boys.' Devon muttered, when the police were out of ear shot. 'you heard the nice policeman, let's go and have some fuckin' fun.'

Some members of the gang glanced nervously at each other. They could tell by the tone of his voice, when he said *some fuckin' fun,* that he meant fuckin' business, nasty fuckin' business. Silently, they headed in the opposite direction towards the Chinaman's shop.

It was young officer Randy Marsh's first day on the beat. Three years of struggling through the police academy, hours of studying, days and days of physical training and now he had finally reached his goal, Officer Marsh of the Chicago PD.

He felt a million dollars walking alongside his new, seasoned partner down the warm, busy street. He wished his old man was still alive to see him all kitted out in his uniform. He would have been so proud. His old man had been a police officer himself, twelve years in the force until he got killed trying to stop a hold up at a convenience store. The maddening thing was his father wasn't even on duty that night. He had just been in the wrong place at the wrong time. Randy had been eight years of age at the time.

But it still didn't stop him wanting to become a cop. He had always wanted to protect and serve his community. It had been his dream, his destiny. To do right by his old man, and to proudly follow in his footsteps.

In this first week, the youngster had been paired up with Officer McCormack, an eighteen stone, one hundred percent white Irish bigamist, with only two years to go before retirement. A tough and uncompromising character, whose motto of survival in this concrete jungle was 'Fight fire with fire, and then some more fire.'

'You got to kick them before they kick you … and kick the fuckers as hard as you can,' the older officer grunted at his new partner, within ten minutes of them getting to know each other.

McCormack wasn't popular with the locals, but he didn't care. He had thick skin and an even thicker baton. He had a job to do, and no one was going to stop him.

'Come on Rookie Marsh,' he laughed out loud at his own sense of humour. 'Let's grab a coffee before we go and lock up some of the natives.'

On first impressions, Randy wasn't quite sure if Officer McCormack was one of the good guys or the bad!

Devon and the gang spread themselves out around the convenience store. It was a trick they had performed a hundred times before all over the city.

On a count of three, two of the boys started arguing loudly at the back of the shop.

'Hey, quit pushing me, you freak.'

'I'll push whoever I feel like.'

Other innocent people in the shop stopped to stare; the owner looked across at them. One of the boys pushed the other one hard in the chest. Accidentally, on purpose, he fell backwards knocking over a stack of cans. There was an almighty racket, canned goods crashing to and rolling across the floor.

The Chinese owner grabbed a baseball bat from under the counter and raced towards the disturbance. 'Get out … you get out, now.' He threatened the youths with the bat.

That was the cue for the others to spring into action. To steal anything, they could get their hands on. In a flash, they began to fill their pockets as fast as they could before piling out into the street.

Devon didn't even try to hide the four-pack of beer he clutched in his powerful grip. He just strolled out through the door, all casual like. The owner, sensing something was going on, turned around to see the newest member of the gang, Travis, aged 15, shoving several packets of cigarettes under his shirt.

Near the front door, the owner grabbed the boy's arm. 'Empty your pockets, thief, thief' he demanded. Their faces were almost touching.

'Get your hands off me,' Travis spat, looking around for support, while grappling to break free.

The owner squeezed his grip. 'I'll call the police.'

Trying to escape, the scared boy lashed out. His elbow smacked the owner square in the face.

Instinctively, the owner retaliated. The baseball bat came down hard on the back of Travis's head.

The boy staggered back into the counter; blood gushed down the side of his face. He dropped the cigarettes onto the ground. The owner whacked him again, across the back. The youth managed to stumble through the door. Once outside he collapsed onto the pavement, blood flowing from his head wound.

The Chinese owner, still holding the bat, followed him out yelling. 'You don't come back … you don't come back.'

A woman passing by bent down to check on the boy. He lay on the asphalt, barely conscious. 'What's happened?' she asked, looking up at the Chinese man.

'Thief … thief.' The shop owner yelled.

Devon was quick on the draw. 'He hit him for nothing … I saw him … He didn't steal anything.'

A small crowd soon gathered around. The owner felt every set of eyes turn to look at him. He retreated back into the shop, locking the door behind him. He turned the sign on the front window from open to closed.

'We can't leave him get away with hitting us kids for nothing,' Devon cried out from the back.

'The boy's right,' an older man grunted.

Two men raced towards the store entrance. They banged on the glass.

'Open this door,' one of them shrieked.

Devon grinned. This was exactly what he'd had in mind when he said 'let's have some fuckin' fun'. He decided to take it up a few levels. He picked up a trash can and threw it through the shop window.

SMASH.

People cheered. A gang of about six people scrambled through the window. The owner tried to protect his property but he was soon overpowered.

A few of them punched and kicked him to the floor. Others were more interested in looting the shelves. More people piled into the shop. Devon opened the cash register and filled his pocket with dollar bills.

Before the owner blacked out, he looked up through the frenzy of punches and kicks at his ransacked shop. A shop he had built up and worked in for most of his life. To make a better life for him and his family.

Out in the street, another member of the gang threw a brick through the window of the electrical shop next door. Even Devon was surprised just how fast the flames of anarchy engulfed the usually quiet street. But the fuse had been lit. It all went off like a giant firework on the Fourth of July. Within twenty minutes, mayhem had engulfed the entire road. Buildings were set on fire, shop windows smashed, cars overturned. Two innocent, Asian teenagers were badly beaten up in a shop doorway.

Devon did his wicked best to keep the flames burning.

The next block over, unaware of the devastation taking place almost in front of them, a laughing and joking Keisha rode on Jerome's back. She climbed down on seeing a cloud of thick, black smoke sailing up into the sky.

Police sirens greeted the loving couple as they turned the corner into the eye of a full-on riot. Individuals rushed past them carrying all manner of items; TV's, CD players, food. Two men struggled past them, carrying a large fridge-freezer still in its original box.

'Jerome, let's get out of here.' Keisha said, leading him away.

'Hang on a minute' He couldn't tear his eyes away from the pandemonium. 'Look.' He pointed at Devon racing through the crowds barking orders. 'I just knew he'd have something to do with it.'

They watched as the thug threw a lump of concrete through a Jeweller's window. The shriek of the alarm system pierced the air. Everyone stopped for a few seconds, before rushing forward like a wave washing up on the shore. A mob like crazed animals dashed through the broken window to grab whatever they could. Powerless to resist, the three female shop assistants raced into the back room and locked the door. Out on the shop floor the store manager tried unsuccessfully to fend off the masses.

Jerome let go of his girlfriend's hand. Looking right and left he rushed forward.

'Jerome, where you going?' she shouted above the noise.

'I'm going to get you what you want.' He headed towards the jewellery shop and clambered in through the smashed window.

'No Jerome, come back.'

Officer Marsh was so scared he almost wet his pants. Him and his older partner had been the first officers at the scene. He couldn't believe what was unfolding before his very eyes. Officer McCormack loved it. He changed into some kind of man possessed. He took great pleasure in using maximum force to try and stop what was going on. He battled through the crowd swinging his baton, hitting everyone within striking distance. The young rookie watched in horror as McCormack cracked the skull of a fourteen-year-old black girl, carrying a vacuum cleaner, with one vicious blow from his truncheon. She fell to the ground unconscious.

'Come on, Rookie Marsh, stop standing there gawking and get some order.' He tugged at his arm.

They raced up the alleyway towards the jewellery store.

Inside the shop, Jerome searched through the glass cabinets for a ring. 'The biggest in the shop,' Keisha's voice played out in his head. He knew he had to be quick before either the police came and nicked them all, or there were no rings left to steal, or both. The manager lay on the floor, hands over his head. A gang of youths beat him with sticks.

'Yes,' Jerome smiled to himself on seeing the ring he wanted. The ring she wanted. It was exactly like she had described it. Large with diamonds and rubies. He smashed the glass with his elbow, and grabbed it, burying it deep into his pocket. He glanced at the other expensive items in the cabinet. But he wasn't interested in anything else, he wasn't greedy. In his mind he wasn't doing this because he was a criminal, he was doing it because he was in love. To him, there was a massive difference.

He fought his way out of the crowded shop. In the street, youths rocked a car back and forth. A loud cheer rose up when the vehicle turned over. Someone threw a homemade petrol bomb, and the automobile burst into flames. More cheers could be heard.

Jerome couldn't believe how nasty the atmosphere had become. Some individuals fought with one another in the street over items they had robbed. Officer McCormack and his rookie raced out of the alleyway. The older officer grabbed a white boy by the throat before digging his baton into the boy's ribs. The officer grinned on hearing the boy's bones crack.

From out of a doorway, Devon watched both officers. He knew this was his chance to get his revenge. The chance he had been waiting for. He hated McCormack. He had been the cop who had arrested his old man and sent him to prison for life after accusing him of killing a police officer at a hold up at a convenience store years before.

As the senior officer laid into an older gentleman who had nothing at all to do with the riots but had only taken an afternoon stroll, the thug raced across and whacked the policeman on the back of the head with an iron bar. McCormack fell like a stone, Devon hit him again. Several gang members raced in and started to boot the copper. Young Officer Marsh stood frozen to the spot.

'Kill the pigs.' Devon yelled out at the top of his voice.

Jerome grabbed him. 'Devon … don't be so stupid.'

Devon pushed him off. 'Get off me … just because you've lost your bottle … go on, get back to your girlfriend.'

The young rookie officer stepped backwards slowly. He wished the ground would open up and swallow him whole. Devon and the mob closed in on him. The cop backed up against the wall of a building. There was no way out.

He withdrew his gun. The crowd closed in. The young policemen had been told during training that the last thing he should ever do was to open fire on a crowd of people. But this wasn't some training routine at the academy. This was life or death, and the odds were stacked against him.

Devon pulled a large knife out of his pocket. He sauntered menacingly forward. The rookie cop closed his eyes and fired. The bullet missed its intended target.

Amongst the chaos, Jerome raced over to Keisha. They held each other tightly.

'You idiot.' She kissed his face. 'You bloody idiot.'

Jerome dropped to his knees again. Around him, people were still running around like headless chickens; smoke bellowed into the sky; alarms pierced the air. Overhead, a police helicopter circled around.

'Keisha … will you marry me?' he rummaged in his pocket for the ring.

'Are you mad?' she laughed nervously.

'Will you?'

'Yes.' She held out her hand. 'Yes … yes.'

The bullet from Officer Marsh's gun, hit the girl full on in the chest. It knocked her backwards. She was dead before she hit the floor.

Everything turned to slow motion in Jerome's world. He crawled over to her. He held her in his arms. Her eyes were lifeless, blood trickled from the side of her mouth. Jerome screamed out. The sirens bellowed down the street.

He turned to see the young rookie officer standing there, gun smouldering in his hand. His entire body shook. Jerome clambered to his feet. He raced across the street, only stopping to rip the knife out of Devon's hand. He barged through a few thugs and buried the blade deep into Officer Marsh's guts. The officer fell to the floor. The youth climbed on top of him and repeatedly stabbed him. 'Keisha … Keisha,' he yelled out each time the knife broke the man's skin.

Devon saw the riot police racing down the alleyway. He went to save his oldest, and perhaps only friend, but the noise of a bullet from the police marksman in the chopper overhead stopped him in his tracks. He looked up and then back at Jerome. His friend was slumped down over the dying officer; half of his head blown away.

The young thug ducked down quickly behind an overturned car. He tried to compose himself. He waited for his chance to escape. The police began to round up everyone they caught, lining them up against the wall. Devon looked down and saw something sparkling in the gutter. He reached out and picked up the large diamond and ruby ring. He pushed it into his jeans, stood up and simply strolled through the chaos towards home.

******

VICTOR

I never imagined this day would ever arrive. It's crept up on me all of a sudden. To be truthful, I'm not sure if I'm happy or sad. For tonight is my last shift on a job that's given me so much pleasure, and a little bit of pain, over the last thirty years or so.

I wonder if, when I finally enter the world of retirement, I'll miss all of the excitement that it's given me along the way. It's been a roller coaster ride with all of its challenges; the mental tests, the physical trials, not to mention the emotional strain. It's been a tough but a very rewarding career. Will I ever make a comeback? No way! I'm not going to be like some fat, over-the-hill, former heavyweight champion of the world who finds it necessary to stagger back into a sweaty boxing ring to hear the clanging sound of the bell one last time.

I ain't no punch-drunk fuckin' mug, right?

I'm quite tired of all the unsociable hours, all the hanging around smokey bars getting pushed around, having to hang about in dark alleyways chilled to the bone. Nah … tonight I will clock in for my last ever shift; give it my best shot as I have always done, and then it's off to Retirement Town. Just me, my slippers and my old Popeye pipe. But all that must wait until tomorrow. Tonight, folks … I still have a job to do, it will be my final curtain call.

Later that night …

I stood inside the Vulcan Arms, looking around menacingly at all of the punters. I thrive on the tension in this bar on a Friday night. The way the adrenaline clings to the walls, a pressure cooker ready to let off steam. Testosterone and bottles of Budweiser mixed with amphetamines and loud music; a complimentary, if dangerous concoction in anyone's book.

Of course, I've changed my appearance. It wouldn't seem right to have a sixty-five-year-old, has-been picking a fight with a twenty-something bloke. Even if the bloke is fat and unfit. I have chosen my disguise carefully. Like Mister Benn in and out of his closet. Or was it a telephone box? Too much irrelevant detail. So, I've decided to use one of my old, favourite characters for tonight's showdown.

Tonight Matthew, I come as a 150lb, wiry framed psychopath from Dublin, Ireland with fast hands and an attitude that could slice a lemon in two.

I breathe in a mouthful of stale, smokey air and prepare myself in readiness for my first assignment. I look about for him.

Yes.

There he is, the cunt, showing off by the bar with his cunty mates. I'll show him. But it's not time yet. I check me watch. Five, four, three, two, one. OK … it's show time. I stroll across the room and bump into him, accidentally on purpose.

'Hey, what the hell?' the heavy-set bloke yells at me above the pounding of the music. 'Watch where you're going, Butt! You nearly spilled my beer.'

Behind him several of his crew snarl at me as if I'm dog shit smeared on the bottom of their new shoes.

'I'll show them,' I whisper to myself. 'Wait and see.'

'Smack the little fucker, Mike,' one of his friends interjected.

I glare at his mate with the big mouth. '*Shame that one isn't on my list*,' I think, biting my bottom lip hard. Regretfully, it's only a one-man contract and it's for the fat chump in front of me.

‘Ain’t you going to say sorry?’ he asks.

I don’t answer. I step back slightly. Too many painful memories and the odd scar from some unpredictable bastard lashing out.

All eyes stare at me. I stand there motionless.

Externally, I’m calm. The first thing I was taught, always look in control. But inside, I am wound tighter than a spring. Like a tiger prowling around its cage. A killing machine with fists of steel and a mind twice as evil as Hitler on a bad hair day.

I can’t wait for it to kick off. Hatred seeps out of my pores; loathing is written all over my face.

‘Well? Apologise, arsehole.’ The bloke's raised voice causes other people at the edge of the bar to stop and stare. I’m now the centre of attention, a feeble David in the throes of getting slaughtered by a big, fat Goliath; I can sense that people are afraid to look at the threatening scene playing out in front of them. But I want them to. I can’t wait to show them what I’m capable of.

I shake my head slowly back and forth in defiance. I can see he’s scared. I don’t take my icey blue eyes off him. Eyes which are cold, lifeless, and full of pent up aggression.

I am proud of my stare. I've perfected it with hours of practice; glaring and sneering at the mirror in the one bedroom of my tiny flat. All of that practice has paid off. I visually see a shiver worming its way up his yellow spine.

He now knows he has made a big mistake. I know, he knows, I know. I smirk and wink at him. His Adam's apple protrudes hard in his throat. He struggles to swallow. He glances around for support. Although the room is packed, in my mind there is only me and him. Beads of sweat drip off his forehead. Adrenaline pumps through my veins faster than an Olympic bob-sleigh team, snaking their way down a black run.

The music pelts out of the speakers. 'Ba Boom … Ba Boom … Ba Boom.'

I wait for him to make the first move. That is rule number 1; unless of course I am playing the role of nightclub bouncer or bent copper. In those cases, no rules apply, hit first, hit hard and as often as you like. They are the kind of jobs I enjoy. There's nothing better than smashing some drunken reveller to pieces outside the emergency exit of a nightclub, while dressed like a gorilla in a monkey suit. Or kicking some cocky demonstrator unconscious in a quiet police cell. Money for old rope.

Back in the crowded bar, I plant my gaze firmly on his face. I wait. I stare and smirk. He knows it's too late for him to back down. It's now or never. I'm reminded of my Da's favourite saying, *'Piss or get off the pot boy.'*

'So, come on fat boy ... piss or get off the fuckin' pot.'

I know he won't; I've done my homework on him. That's why I've lasted so long in this occupation. I'm a professional, see, who takes his career seriously. There is no room for amateurs in this bear pit of an arena.

I always read all the notes supplied about my proposed targets. No stone is left unturned. And I read that this one is all talk. Nothing but a heartless bully, until the chips are down. And at this moment in time, his chips are deep fried and covered in salt and fuckin' vinegar.

'Hold my beer.' He hands it to his friend with the big mouth. He turns back towards me. 'Are you looking for a fight, Butt?' He pokes me in the chest.

Those are the last words he mutters this fateful night. The half empty Bud bottle connects beautifully with the side of his big, chubby face, breaking his jaw in three places. I love the thud sound that glass makes when it connects with its human target. There's nothing that can describe it, no words, no phrases, nothing. I bet even bleedin' Shakespeare would have struggled, no fuck him, I bet even Bono, yeah, Bono, would fail to capture the sheer majesty of it.

At first the shock on everyone's face is surreal. For a split second no one says a word, or moves a muscle. They stand rooted to the spot. The fat boy spits blood and numerous teeth onto the floor. He staggers forward. I hit him again just for the craic of it. This time on the other side; I think it's only fair to even up his newly deformed features.

Then the real fun starts. A girl screams. Her shrieks sail high up to the ceiling. Tables are overturned, punches are thrown, and kicks rain into thin air. A mass brawl breaks out; everyone wants to kill the wiry nutcase who has carried out the cowardly act.

But I'm gone, see. Like Keyser Soze. Disappeared off into the night. So, while the bouncers wade in and the police sirens wail, I'm outside the kebab shop, just a mature gentleman with icy blue eyes and a liking for spicy food.

"Put plenty of garlic sauce on it, my man, plenty of garlic sauce."

My first mission of the night has been successfully completed.

'Hit them hard,' my old Da told me when I was growing up. 'Listen my boy … hit them hard, hit them once. Never worry about the consequences, never look back … just go and get something to eat … need to keep your energy levels up.'

Billy Edwards … Billy the bully Edwards is crossed off my list. And I've escaped scot-free … well, except for a spot of heartburn and probably a fiery ring in the morning.

Now, it's time to move out and move on. I'm still expected to make my nightly quota, even though it's my last shift.

No rest for the King of Chaos, that's the name I gave myself … good isn't it? … the King of Chaos … Oooooh, I'm in the mood now.

Next stop, Clapham Common … 7.45pm, it's dark. This is where the perverts and the nonces cruise about, looking for brief and anonymous encounters of the sick kind. Grown men hiding in bushes, playing toy soldiers. Disgusting.

Amongst the undergrowth, we wait near the toilets. Yes, I'm part of a gang now. Evil can take many forms. Seven of us, from up the East End, hide, heads freshly shaved, Doc Martens ready, ox-blood polished to a military finish and barking for action. I love the gang assignments. Should have seen us at the European Football Championships in Holland. Evil thugs, bent on causing bedlam. I'm ashamed of the things I did, proper ashamed! But sometimes one must do what one's been commanded to do.

Hold up, look lively, here's one. Let's call him Big Dave, no, no, no … Big Ron, about forty-five. Smug, little git in his corduroy slacks and hush puppies. His Trouble, now, probably back in their gaff, cooking up pork chops and garlic bread. He probably made a lame-arsed excuse about nipping out for some wine or cigarettes. Dirty fuckin' fag!

What'd you say, boys? You what? Me … cos it's my last gig before me big off … are you serious? I tell you what you lot are … you're a bunch of sentimental bastards is what you are. Cheers boys … let's make it a good one then, hey?

I walk from the shadows … he sees me. He nods. I nod back. I force my lips into a smile; he smiles back. I feel his eyes crawling all over my body. It makes my skin creep; Control, control.

‘Excuse me Gov, you haven’t got a spark for me leather bag,’ I says in me cockney accent.

‘Yes of course, he says, offering me a light.

‘Cheers, nice one,' I says.

'Cold tonight' he says.

'Yeah, brassic' I says.

I eyeball him. I smell the desire on his breath. His hands shake. His fingers touch my face. I clench. He looks into my eyes. I stare at the ground to conceal the pure hatred welling up inside of me. His fingers move down my tee-shirt, lightly stroking my nipples. I count to ten very, very, very slowly.

His hands explore further down my body. Lower and lower. I feel his lust in his every action. I masquerade my heavy breathing as false passion; He goes down on his knees in front of me. I look back towards the bushes. My pack waits, eyes red, fangs dripping spittle.

He tries to undo me zip. Ooooooo that’s him fucked. ‘Come here you fucking nonce.’ In one movement I grab him by the neck and spin him around. My pack of pit-bulls appear. 'You ain’t going anywhere.'

BOOM

A doc marten boot connects with his groin. A beauty. He slumps to the ground and curls up in a ball, crying like a fuckin' baby. Blows rain down on him. A boot connects with his open mouth; teeth shatter. We kick, we punch, we stamp, I slice. We cheer … his body lies lifeless. I walk away, leaving my lads to finish him off.

'Well done Geezers! I'm going to miss you bunch of muppets.'

Bloke in bar - tick. Joyrider, hit and run … or hit and drive away as fast as I could – four victims, extra bonus for that. Tick, tick. Ching, ching. Mugged some businessman, nicked his phone. Easy money - tick, and now the queer in the park - BIG tick. And now I'm off to 'meet and greet' my last ever victim … TAXI!!!

Look, before you judge me, I don't really like violence. I don't … I was just born into it, see.

I remember … I was seven, or eight … dinner, kitchen table … me, my dad, and my mam … I sat in the middle of them. He'd been out. Drunk, itching for an argument. I hated him when he was like that. We'd sat there, eating away.

'This is lovely mam,' I broke the silence.

‘Thank you, Victor,’ she replied. ‘Pass the gravy,’ my mother asked my father. That’s all it was … ’Pass the gravy, love. Pass the gravy.’

‘I’ll get it mam,’ I said.

‘No, you won’t boy, sit still.’ He stared at her. ‘what did you say, woman?’ I could smell the beer on his breath as he spat the words out in her face.

‘Pass the gravy, love. It’s next to you,’ her voice shook a little.

There was another silence, more toxic than before. I looked down at the table, like kids do. My father stood up.

BANG

He punched my mother full force in the face. His ring … a big fuckin’ sovereign … the size of a brazil nut … sliced the lid of her eye. She shot across the kitchen floor, blood everywhere. Then do you know what he did? … do you know what that pig of a man did then? … he poured the gravy over her head. Blood and gravy. I was too afraid to move, too afraid to look up.

‘I’m off to the pub,’ he grunted and walked out.

25 stitches she had. Scar on her eye until the day she died. It wasn’t just her he dished it out to. I took my fair share along the way.

The tele's too loud, boy I'm trying to sleep.

BANG

Did you tip pop on the settee, boy?

BANG

Did you eat all the biscuits, boy?

BANG

Did you do this, boy?

BANG

Did you do that, boy?

BANG … BANG … BANG … Fuckin' BANG.

It was a tough childhood. I hated being at home. On the other hand, I hated going to school as well. I bunked off most days. But … but I did like football … I was quite good at it …

'Like a little Georgie Best.' my sports teacher Mister Brown told me.

He got me a district trial at the park. The only boy in my school. I begged my dad to come and watch.

'I'll see.' he grunted.

The day of the big game, he hadn't shown up. That first half I had a blinder, two goals. First one, top right-hand corner, whoosh.

Second goal, around the keeper and slotted it into an empty net. Half time, Mister Brown gave me the thumbs up.

'Going great, Victor, great … same second half and you'll not only be in the district, but maybe even in the Welsh team.'

I shook with excitement. I couldn't stop smiling. But then … but then, he turned up. My dad with his drunken mates. Flagons of Strongbow in their hands. I could hear them abusing the other fathers. But I tried to concentrate, I wanted to show my dad what I could do.

The whistle blew. I received the ball on the half way line. I beat one player, boosh … beat another and then a third, boosh. The full back came at me, I nutmegged him, sweet as a nut, mind the pun … only the goalie to beat. I did my trademark dummy swerve, one way, then the other way, but I kicked my own feet. I fell head over tit. I jumped back up but the goalie had wrapped his hands around the ball.

'Penalty ref … definitely a penalty,' my father screamed out from the touchline.

'No, dad, I tripped.'

'Ref … penalty … come on … you fuckin' blind or what?'

'It was my fault dad,' I pleaded.

He wasn't listening. He marched onto the field.

'No, dad, no.'

Straight up to the referee.

'Please, dad, no … it was my fault, I tripped.'

'Oi ref.' he shouted.

BANG.

Mister Brown raced on to stop my dad kicking the helpless man.

BANG.

He got it too.

BANG.

BANG.

BANG fuckin' BANG

Silence.

Match abandoned. Ref in hospital. Dad arrested. Mister Brown left the school. My football career abandoned. My life abandoned.

Silence.

He gave me his ring on his deathbed

'This is for you, son,' he said. Like it was a fuckin' war medal. The fuckin' bully. He should have been on my list for what he did to my mother and me.

Of course, it affected me. When I reached a certain age, I swapped my football boots, for these. My knuckles got me the nickname – Victor the Knuckles.

I started to go and watch Cardiff. Followed them everywhere … CAR AD IFF … CAR AD IFF … CAR AD IFF

Your gonna get your fuckin' head kicked in …

Your gonna get your fuckin' head kicked in …

Your gonna get your fuckin' head kicked innnnnnnnnn.

I loved it, see, and not to appear big headed, I was good at. Good at all the violence, see. Fit body, fit mind. Vicious, vicious beyond belief. I wasn't afraid of anyone or anything. Got me in a stack of trouble.

But then I met her … Gloria.

She is … no, she was … she was … my …Well, we met in our mid-twenties … lovely, sexy, funny she was. She had been brought up proper, like. Eighteen months … eighteen glorious months we spent together. I did my best to change. I didn't want to screw it up. She opened up a new world for me. She wasn't some council estate slag. More middle class. I stopped going to the footy, I did. She took me to art galleries instead. To be honest most of it was shite, but I said I liked them. I think she knew I didn't. But then … but then, she took me to the theatre. Yes me, Victor the Knuckles Norman. I … bought a suit to go. I bought a fuckin' suit. I didn't think I would like it, but it was wonderful. The best thing I had ever seen … ever heard. I was hooked; shell shocked.

I wanted to be with her for the rest of my life. I wanted us to be together. I wanted us to have a family. I wanted to treat my kid, my boy, the way I should have been treated by my old man. So, I bought a ring; booked a posh restaurant. One of her favourites. I sat there full of nerves; sweating all over. I had it all planned out. Get down on one knee … like in the movies. Romantic like.

I knew she was going to say … say … yes.

Then they came in. Rugger boys. Three of them sitting on the next table over. Loud and proud, laughing and swearing, and smoking and singing, and laughing and swearing, and smoking and singing, and laughing and swearing, and smoking and singing.

I just wanted it to be perfect. I went over and asked them to quiet down a little. 'Look boys … it's a special night for me … for us. Keep it down a little please,' I almost pleaded.

They didn't listen. Louder and louder, they got. I gripped the wine bottle in my hand.

"Don't worry about them, Victor … it's a lovely night … let's just enjoy it.' She smiled at me.

I wasn't listening. I gripped the bottle tighter. My blood boiling; my knuckles white. The red mist descended over me.

Silence.

I don't remember anything else about that night … nothing.

Two years, that's what I got. Swansea bastard nick as well. Fuckin' Jacks.

After a few weeks, Gloria came to see me. I was so pleased to see her. 'I'm sorry, Gloria,' I said, 'so sorry. I will change. I will. I love you. I'll make it up to you when I'm out. I promise.'

She kind of smiled. A strange look in her eyes; distant. Then she spoke. Her words hit me harder than any punch or boot I had ever taken in my life. 'Victor … I've found someone else … we're moving away together … I never want to see you again … bye.'

Bye.

Bye.

FUCKING BYE …

I watched her walk away. I would have passed the gravy to her … I would have passed the gravy to her for the rest of my life.

From that moment on, I knew I didn't need pussy to get me hard. Violence was my only mistress. It was all the fuckin' sex I needed. The best fuckin' orgasm in the world.

When I got out, my life spiralled out of control. I became more vicious and it wasn't pretty. I fucked up again, big style, you don't need to know the details. My barrister told me I'd get an eight stretch. I resigned myself for the worst, but then the letter arrived, recorded delivery.

It looked odd. But it hadn't been written like a normal letter. The words were cut out of a newspaper like a serial killer sending a clue to the FBI.

It said … *'They' were impressed with my work, and they would like to employ me. And if I did a good job, and kept my mouth shut, all charges would be dropped.'*

However, there were certain guidelines. Rules I had to abide too. It meant I had to change. No more being a hot head. I had to control my anger; control my aggression. Learn how to strike fast and then disappear. I thought, 'I could cope with that.' I agreed, charges dropped. Back of the fuckin' net.

Then, every Tuesday morning a plain, brown envelope arrived with a list of "victims" and a bundle of cash. How great that my passion was now my full-time job. Like an overpaid footballer, getting paid to kick a football around a patch of grass. Now here I was, getting cash for causing chaos.

I reckon it had something to do with the government. Well it makes perfect sense, doesn't it? Well doesn't it? Look, if we don't have violence where would the economy be? There would be no need for so many policemen, nurses, ambulance drivers, doctors and of course members of the gutter press; they love a good headline. Not to mention judges, lawyers, politicians, TV news reporters and all the rest of society's parasites who feed off the misfortunes of others. Those are the real blood suckers, not me! I was just trying to earn a decent living. I made a packet. But as per usual, I wasted it all on gambling, cheap booze and cheaper women. I had a fuckin' great time. Where did it all go wrong Georgie boy; where did it all go wrong?

And now I'm on my way to my last ever assignment.

‘Yes drive, it’s Blossom Grove number 4. Yeah, it’s probably the one with the fridge in the garden … fucking comedian as well hey?’

You won’t believe who my last character is. Fuckin’ hell, you won’t … my last role ever, before a life of old age is a horrible, sadistic, loser of a husband with the world on his shoulders and a belly full of beer. The irony.

‘Yes drive … I’ll get out here. How much? Fuckin’ hell, drive, I’m subsidising half of Poland as well, am I? OK … ok and no, you can’t keep the change.’

I saunter down the street, it's a typical working-class area. I can smell the poverty and desperation. I enter the house and I see her lying there. She’s fast asleep on the settee. She looks so peaceful with the light from the television flickering on her face. She looks almost angelic, so peaceful.

Time to get into character. I pull out my shirt and get into drunken mode. I’m ready.

‘Where’s me fuckin’ food bitch?’ I spit the words in a thick Liverpudlian accent into her shocked face. My hatred sticks to her skin like a two-day old rash. The best part is, I'm not even hungry. Us scousers are so witty at times.

'Mammy … Mammy.'

I look over my shoulder. 'Oh no … a small boy,' I turn back into character. 'Don't worry about mummy … get back into bed la … or you'll be fuckin' next.'

He scurries off. I spin back to face the woman. She's crawling away. My boot catches her in the rib cage. I hear it crack. She slumps onto the carpet, winded; wriggling around on the floor, yelping like a wounded dog just hit by a car.

'Oh no, you don't, bitch.' I push her into the cheap coffee table. Ornaments rain down on top of her crumpled body. Blood drips from her mouth, snot runs from her nose. 'You dirty cow.' I slap her.

'Mummy, are you OK?'

'I told you once la … it's the strap for you.' I take off my belt and head towards the stairs. 'That's it la, get in your room and don't dare come out. I'll be up to deal with you later.'

I turn back. 'That's it, bitch, get in that kitchen and make me my scran.'

I take the list of "victims" out of my pocket and put a line through her name. I will always remember her name … Helen Denise Bond. I know the brief said just rough her up a bit, break a few ribs, maybe a broken nose. But what the hell. I take the ring out of my pocket; I look up to the heavens. 'This is for you, dad.'

I find her cowering by the cooker, hair a mess, and face fixed firmly to the floor. I grab her by her dyed roots and pull her up to my level. I stare into her face. I'm surprised that her eyes aren't filled with tears. In fact, her eyes are similar to mine, cold, calculating, and icey blue. I am even more taken aback when a grin appears on the edge of her mouth.

I glance down and see her clutching a bread knife in her left hand.

'What're you going to do with that bitch?'

Before I have time to react, she stabs out in anger. It penetrates my skin; a gaping wound appears in my abdomen. She spits in my face and repeats the action again, and again. In and out it goes, again, in and out; I am powerless and too confused to resist.

It is my turn to fall to the floor, trying desperately to stem the flow of blood, which seeps out onto the dirty linoleum. I feel a shivering cold creeping through my body. I reach out to grab her ankle. She moves away, stepping sharply onto my exposed fingers. In another part of the kitchen, the small boy emerges. Strangely he now appears much older than his nine years of age. He has a grin on his face as if it was Christmas morning. The boy kicks me in the side. 'Stab him again mammy … stab him again.'

I start to shake. The woman puts the knife down and reaches into her apron pocket. She slowly pulls out a piece of paper with six names on it. Five have been crossed out. She shrugs her shoulders in a very 'I'm so sorry sir, but I'm only doing my job' sort of way. She leisurely crosses my name out in black biro ink.

The small boy hands me a card. On it the words are printed in big, bold lettering. I squint to see what it says. I hear myself reading the words: -

'Thanks for all of your outstanding years of service ... much appreciated ... signed ...'

I feel weak; I try to read the signature but the room suddenly goes black.

THE END

Thank you and all that jazz!!!

Firstly, I must say a gigantic and colossal 'thank you' to **Rhiannon Owens-Sullivan** who actually 'volunteered' to sort out my crap spelling and grammar. She didn't know what she was letting herself in for!

'Rhiannon, I owe you lots of beers and some nice grub when all this lockdown madness is over' x

Also, I would like to acknowledge the input from **Neil Maidman, Paul Black, Callum Kemp-Jones, Andrew Lennon** and lots of the cast from **Gurnwah Productions** who helped colour in some of these fables and personalities when we were rehearsing bits and pieces of them for our stage plays.

I've heard lots of tales and anecdotes about my town and its crazy old characters over the years. Some of them appear in this book, although I may have stretched the truth even further than it was actually stretched at the time!!!! So, I would like to thank the individuals who consciously, or unconsciously, sparked off little bushfires in my imagination.

And finally, after all these lost years, I would still like to thank **Mister Fulgoni** for that Scollop….the best scollop I've ever tasted

Stay Free

Bunko

Other titles by Anthony Bunko

- The Tale of the Shagging Monkeys – Trippin'
- Two Shagging Monkeys – The Siege of El Rancho
- The Belt of Kings
- Boy, Girl, Fruitcake, Flower (renamed – TV, Tarot Cards and George bloody Clooney)
- Working up to the Slaughterhouse
- *Demons and Cocktails - Stuart Cable's autobiography*
- *Hugh Laurie Biography*
- *Hugh Jackman Biography*
- *2 Hard to Handle – the autobiography of Mike Spikey Watkins*
- *Deadwalker*
- Dic Penderyn and the Merthyr Rising.
- Lord Forgive me but I was a Bullshit Consultant
- *Ma'am Anna – Anna Rodriguez's autobiography*
- *Nerves of Steele – the Story of Phil Steele*
- The Boy who Cried Sheep
- The Wizard of GurnOZ

Printed in Poland
by Amazon Fulfillment
Poland Sp. z o.o., Wrocław

59515109R00146